# WHERE DO STORIES COME FROM?

BY

KATHLEEN GLASSBURN

Where Do Stories Come From?
Copyright: Kathleen Glassburn
Published: September 2018
ISBN: 978-1-7324395-0-4

This book was published with the assistance of Self-Publishing Relief, a division
of Writer's Relief.

# Contents

*For Sam and Stephanie*
*who are busy living their own stories*

# WHERE DO STORIES COME FROM?

When I started taking classes and workshops in fiction writing several decades ago, I always wanted to ask the author, *Where did that story come from?*

Trying to be inconspicuous, I stayed quiet. No one else asked either. Would it be impolite? Would it lessen the process to know what sent a writer off on a particular story? Would it take away from the art of the piece?

Everyone was too busy deconstructing the plot, looking for relevant imagery, telling the author in a short first statement what was good about his or her story and most often, in lengthy detail, why the story didn't work.

Recently, I released my first novel—*Making It Work.* The question I'm continually asked is: *How much is autobiographical?* My standard answer is: *About 80% of it is fictional.* One friend said: "You married your high school sweetheart, right?" *Yes.* "And, he was in the Navy during Vietnam?" *Yes.* "And, you lived in Long Beach, California?" *Yes.* Her eyebrows raised and she shrugged off any more questions. I attempted an explanation of the fictional process as I understand it, but she was dismissive.

These two situations: always wondering where other writers got their stories, and my friend, a scientific type who focuses on factual evidence, set me off on this project. My first collection of short stories.

Fiction writing is a mysterious, magical endeavor. Often, I don't know exactly where some parts of a story come from; however, I do know the initial spark that sent me off on a written exploration, eventually ending with a complete work.

It's an adventure.

# BIDING TIME

*Another friend asked if I would like to accompany a group of assisted-living residents on a field trip to the Woodland Park Zoo in Seattle. She was a paid companion for one of the residents. I'd never visited a facility of this kind and was curious as well as wanting to be helpful. I remember thinking: Who knows, maybe a story will come from this. When I'm doing something that interrupts my writing time this thought often surfaces. It is important for writers to put aside their work occasionally, in order to experience new activities that just might inspire a spark that just might end up in a full-blown flame.*

*The elderly gentleman in my story, while patterned after my friend's companion, took on a life of his own. The other characters came from my imagination. Some of the action came from my observations of residents and visitors to the zoo on that sunny day.*

*The one event that came from my past is: Duncan lying awake while his friends are sound asleep. When I was ten years old and staying at an overnight summer camp several of us, accompanied by three counselors, hiked to a "haunted house" where we rolled out our sleeping bags, made a campfire, and slept under the stars after we'd roasted hot dogs, eaten s'mores, sang lots of songs, and told ghost stories. By midnight, everyone else had fallen asleep while I was wide awake, wishing I could drift off, but too aware of the abandoned building in the background. I never forgot that miserable night, and in later years it made me think about what it must be like for an elderly person who has lost all his or her friends, who is all alone, staring at the stars. Duncan is that kind of sensitive soul. Waiting...*

*"Biding Time" was published under the name Kay Harris.*

# Biding Time

Published by *SLAB*, 2007

Last night, Duncan Ainsworth did the same thing he's done every night since moving into Brookside Manor. Stared at the black holes in the ceiling tile and waited. The nurses say he can have "a little something to bring on sleep," but Duncan behaves so they don't slip it to him. He knows what meds he takes. They're for his problem and that's all. He doesn't need anything numbing him. His body's finally going but his brain's as good as ever. Not brilliant. He doesn't claim that. Still, he had another article published in The Messenger a few months back: "Changes to the Mowbray Waterfront in the '50s." And, the editor wants more. If Duncan wasn't so damned tired, he could honor that request; however, it takes all his energy to keep out of a wheelchair and off of a walker. There's nothing left for an article. Plus, someone would have to take him out to do research. Much as he loves her, Duncan can't tolerate his daughter Edie's hovering.

Yesterday Duncan turned ninety-eight. He walked around the activity room and conversed with his guests, all of whom were most impressed with the bouquet of late-blooming roses Edie brought from the garden at his old house.

Gladys Funkhauser, a long-time resident of The Manor, went on about them for a good five minutes. "There's yellow and pink and even red!" she said, clapping hands under her lipstick-besmeared chin. Gladys reached out to hang onto Duncan's arm just as he did a quick sidestep.

After the hoopla, Edie boxed up the leftover salmon-shaped cake. Duncan used to fish—just for fun. Half the belly and tail remained. It had been an orange monstrosity that reminded him of those awful marshmallow peanut things. Actually, it was a tinted vanilla cover-up for his favorite fudge. He marched up to Edie as she struggled with the carton and said, "I have something to tell you, Edith."

"Are you OK, Daddy? The party wasn't too much?" She stews about Duncan's health nonstop. Their conversations center around the food forced upon him and the regularity of his eliminations. Popping two fingers covered with lumps of frosting in her mouth, his daughter stared at him with round blue eyes set in cheeks as plump as when she was in diapers.

"I'm fine—just fine. I merely want to say thank you. And, good-by."

"Good-by?"

"Tonight's the night. Call tomorrow. I'll be gone."

"Oh, Daddy, that's nonsense. You're going to make it to at least a hundred."

"No, Edie. Prepare yourself. My time has come. You're always hearing about it—people lasting for the visit of a long-lost child, or another Christmas, or one more birthday—then pffffft, they're gone. This is it. My one more birthday. Now, it's over."

Edie made sure she got every last piece of that cake packed in the carton. Didn't even leave one bite for the nurses. Then she bellowed to all those still gathered, "Duncan Ainsworth is going to make it to at least a hundred!"

She did leave the roses. Petals had already fallen on the table—they don't seem to last long by September. In a softer voice, hugging her father, Edie said, "Talk to you tomorrow," before frumping out to her car with the cake.

Duncan thought, No way. This is definitely the end of the line.

*** 

Last night, he folded hands over his chest, closed his eyes, and stayed quiet. Under the room rumbles and his own steady breathing, he thought he heard a cricket chirping—probably somebody's monitor. "I'm ready," he whispered. "Come and get me."

This morning, there was Duncan Ainsworth, jarred awake and prodded to go on their damned field trip. "It's our special birthday present to you," said Mandy, the one in charge of keeping inmates busy at The Manor. She was taking some of them to the zoo. Made a big deal about it. Due to the new mini-bus, this was the first excursion ever, and weren't they oh so lucky to be chosen to attend. Duncan glanced around the lobby at three in wheelchairs, two leaning against walkers, and only Mrs. Wilder and himself able to sit in regular armchairs. With her hands shoved under the cushion for leverage, Mrs. Wilder acted like she might bolt at any moment.

The attendants had hustled participants through breakfast in order to provide plenty of time for boarding. Consequently, Duncan's stomach was doing one of its clenching routines and he munched on TUMS trying to settle it. At least I'm sitting in a regular chair and walking unassisted, not dependent on some fool metal contraption to get me from point A to point B, he thought. Embarking was set for 9:00 a.m. "It's nigh on time to depart," he informed Mrs. Wilder, who didn't respond, her head cocked to one side as she watched the chattering volunteers come in.

Mandy told Mrs. Wilder and Duncan, "You're going to have to ride when we get to the zoo. Your volunteer will push you."

"I'm perfectly able to get around on my own two feet," Duncan said.

Mrs. Wilder raised herself, grunting. Mandy nudged her back in the armchair, and turned to Duncan. "Mr. Ainsworth, I know that. But it's the rule. If you were to fall, I'd be out on my ear. You wouldn't want that to happen, would you?"

Duncan allowed as how he wouldn't choose to be the cause of her termination, but said, "Only this once. I won't ride in one of those buggies on a regular basis. Put that in my file. Duncan Ainsworth is one hundred percent mobile."

Mrs. Wilder didn't say one thing. She could carry half her weight if they had to evacuate The Manor. Yet, without someone to direct her, she'd never find the door.

Duncan's assigned volunteer, Bonnie by name, commenced talking. She said, "I've never been to Brookside Manor. Lived around the block for years. Decided I should come and try to help out. Have you been here long?" She waited for his answer, alert as a pup.

"Too long," he told her. Three months ago they hospitalized him—bloody stool. Lost a lot of weight. His son, Baxter, the busy banker, insisted on more supervision. To Duncan, that sounded like a toddler. He'd stayed in his house, all alone, tending the roses, for twenty-six years. "Yesterday was my ninety-eighth birthday," he told Bonnie. "And this is where it'll all end."

"Oh my. You were born in 1900. The whole twentieth century to tell about."

Duncan thought, Couldn't she come up with something better? Didn't she know that everyone who discovered his birth year immediately made that kind of comment? But he forgave her. She was such a pretty little thing. Silky blonde hair and brown eyes. He liked that combination. It brought to mind a Cocker Spaniel he had once. His volunteer had a dimple in one cheek, too. When she wasn't making the effort, it disappeared. The more he watched those brown eyes, the more they reminded him of Gildie, only in the last year, when the Vet found her tumor. His dog had looked at Duncan with sadness in her face, trying to wag, hurting so much and barely able to move. At last, he had to put her down.

This Bonnie was trying so hard. Why was a lovely young woman like her in The Manor's waiting room anyway?

The two sat and chitter-chatted for a good long while. It was past 9:00 before they even started to load. Duncan wondered how the organizers planned to get the whole shebang to the zoo, wheel around there, pack them all up, and arrive back at The Manor for noon dinner. He concluded it was their problem and he was just going along for the ride.

Bonnie said, "That's a most becoming jacket, Mr. Ainsworth. It looks so nice with your white hair. Brown tweed'll never go out of style." The jacket, a leftover from his classroom days, had served him well. Thankfully, Baxter delivered a whole armload of clean clothes on Duncan's birthday. His son stayed ten minutes before rushing off to the next appointment. Didn't even get a piece of cake. Nonetheless,

Duncan was glad he had fresh apparel because he couldn't stand it when old people forgot to take care of themselves.

"It should last as long as I do," he said, and put on his matching peaked cap.

The two watched while attendants struggled with those permanently in wheelchairs, rolling them on the platform elevator, strapping their wheels, and jerking them along before coming to rest at seat level. He wondered what would happen if a chair broke loose and zoomed right back through those automatic double glass doors into the lobby. It could be someone's biggest thrill in years. Of course, most of them probably wouldn't be roused enough to experience the ride.

Mrs. Trimble's head flopped to one side, eyes closed. Her little feet, in pink slippers with posies embroidered on the fronts, hung—toes crossed. She never even startled when they bumped her onto the lift, bounced her up, and stuck her in the back corner of the bus facing Mr. Limkin, the only other man on their trip. He had waxy white skin and a perpetually smiling mouth. Duncan wondered what in God's name Mr. Limkin had to smile about. He didn't dare consider why the man was so pallid.

Mrs. Trimble lolled the whole trip. Duncan decided she didn't have a notion of ever leaving her room.

Mr. Limkin stared straight ahead, his clenched grin never wavering. After the field trip was over, one of the nurses asked if he had a good time. Duncan saw him blink twice and wondered if that meant "yes" or "no."

He climbed up into the new bus on his own steam. No one hauled his arms from the front, or pushed his back from the rear, or reached down and guided his feet onto the ledge of each step to make sure Duncan made it inside. When he got to his seat, first one in the front, nobody came along and grabbed him, saying "One—two—three," and hoisted him into place because he'd slid, cock-eyed, against the corner.

Duncan sat straight up next to the window with Bonnie beside him on the aisle.

As soon as they were belted and ready to take off, she leaned over and said, "Mr. Ainsworth, you certainly get around well."

"I know," he said, "and I intend to keep it that way."

In spite of the brand new upholstery, Duncan could detect that odor. "I apologize for the smell in here," he whispered, his mouth close to Bonnie's flower-scented hair. "They've lost control."

She smiled and her dimple flickered. "No big deal, Mr. Ainsworth. I don't mind a bit."

By the time they arrived at the zoo, it was after 10:00. Attendants hauled out chairs and issued one to Duncan. Once they finished the disembarking procedure and hit the trail, he and Bonnie brought up the rear. They were right behind Mrs. Trimble, whose cheek bounced on her scrunched-up shoulder as they crossed every hump in the path. Her volunteer, a woman with a broad backside Duncan and Bonnie could barely see around, kept trying to get Mrs. Trimble's attention with remarks about the marigolds blooming away and the baby zebra hiding behind a bush. These efforts were in vain.

Everyone clustered together at the exhibits while the pushers jockeyed chairs in position for advantageous views. Duncan thought, At wheelchair level it's like being a little kid. Those fool fences hit you right across the eyes.

Mr. Limkin was as happy gazing at the penguins as he'd been staring at the door handle in the mini-bus on the trip over.

Mrs. Wilder mumbled and had to be restrained each time they stopped. Duncan thought he detected a flash of recognition when they came to the gorilla playground.

After almost an hour, the group had visited three exhibits. Duncan said to Bonnie, "The roses are still out. I saw them from the entrance. Do you suppose we could go look at the garden?"

"I saw them, too."

"We used to grow roses, you know. Had fifty bushes and quite a few climbers at our old house. I'd rather be with the flowers than these poor caged creatures."

"I'll ask permission," she said, and engaged Duncan's brake.

Bonnie received the OK, as long as they were back to the mini-bus by 11:30. Thus, the pair made their escape. Of course, it was late in the season and the blooms were waning, if not downright bedraggled. Even so, sunshine warmed their shoulders as Duncan and Bonnie took in the colors.

There was a bed of rich, dark-red Mr. Lincolns. "I'll bet his sitting room wallpaper was of that tone," Duncan said. "The Sterling Silvers make a nice contrast to some of the deeper shades, don't you think?"

"I do."

"I'm glad there's a good showing of Peace." Duncan noted how the pink-edged yellow blossoms were intact. "That was my late wife Merrill's favorite. It was the first bush we ever planted together."

Bonnie patted his arm. After a minute, she said, "I'm not much of a gardener with only one rosebush in my yard. It's kind of orange-colored and scraggly-looking."

"Could be a Tropicana. It probably needs pruning. Around March first you do that."

Duncan proceeded to tell Bonnie about his years teaching history at the community college.

Which led her to ask, "Have you traveled much, Mr. Ainsworth?"

"When I retired, Merrill and I did a lot of touring—Europe, Asia, even Russia. After she died in '72, I did go once with a group from Mowbray's Botanical Society—found that a night boatride on the Seine, passing the Eiffel Tower glimmering from base to top, was too much without her hand in mine." He paused, studying the Peace roses. "About the time my journeys ended, though, the curator position at our museum opened and no one was better qualified than me."

Bonnie talked about volunteering in the elementary school, helping slow readers one-on-one. "After Markie's death, I couldn't go back."

"Markie?"

"My seven-year-old son. He had problems turning letters around. I tutored in his class." She stopped as if wondering what else should be said. Then, "At the lake…Markie swam out too far."

Bonnie was sitting on the grass next to Duncan's chair. This time he put his hand on her shoulder and gave a little pat. "We lost a child, too. John was barely five."

Bonnie didn't ask how John died and Duncan didn't want to talk about the boy's illness. He was feeling better than he had in months. Why spoil it? He'd rather quietly wait, enjoying the garden and the last of the roses.

While riding back to Brookside Manor, Duncan told Bonnie about an article he wanted to write: "The First Fishing Fleet Out of Mowbray."

She figured they could get special permission to go back to his museum and to the library. "As long as we bring a wheelchair."

A look of disgust settled on Duncan's face.

"Following the rules is very important to Mandy," Bonnie said.

"That's for sure."

***

With the big outing, Duncan should be sleepy tonight, but he's not. After a short while, staring at the black holes in the ceiling, he starts thinking about the fishing fleet. As long as I'm awake, I might as well concentrate on something productive. Bonnie'll come for me next Monday, to start my research. After I do my work, I'm going to take her to the bakery for some double fudge cake—none of that orange frosting stuff. She seems like a reasonable young woman. Maybe I can convince her to leave their wheelchair in the car.

Still waiting for sleep to find him, Duncan turns to memories of camping trips when he was a boy. The gang would hike five miles out of town to the old Guffey place—the "haunted house." He was always jittery, but what would the fellas have said if he'd stayed home? Duncan was sure they never knew about his nerves. Every time he stumbled over a branch or startled from an owl's hoot, he managed to cover up his feelings.

Once to their destination, the boys plopped bedrolls around the fire—not too close to the house—roasted wienies, told scary stories, and fell asleep by dwindling embers.

Everyone except Duncan.

He'd lie there, staring at the stars and listening to the snores around him, wondering if he was ever going to slip off like his pals. The house loomed behind him, and he was sure there'd been a face in a window or a movement on the dilapidated front porch. He pleaded with the dark sky and stars, If there's a God up there, let me go to sleep. I'm down here…alone. There's no one to talk to.

Eventually, long after all the rest, Duncan drifted away, too.

## *TESTAMENT*

*When I was a kid our family visited my maternal grandmother and grandfather in Park Rapids, Minnesota at least once, sometimes twice, a year. I was the oldest, with a younger brother. My boy cousin was the same age as my brother and he had a sister who was the youngest of our quartet. I don't remember us all hanging out together that much, but I do remember a time when we hiked to the "haunted house" about a mile from my grandparents' cottage. The children aren't anything like my brother and my cousins. The older girl is probably quite a bit like I was as a child—very responsible, a rule follower, and not particularly brave. We weren't Catholic, but Catholicism often shows up in my writing. It's probably because I can write more conflict than if I used our more lenient Episcopalian membership as a religious theme. Also, my father's family were Irish Catholics who left the Church long before I was born. The incidents in the story are all made up with the exception of the false teeth in the cellar of the old abandoned house. We saw those teeth sitting on a work bench and ran like the dickens. I wonder who left them there. That could be another story. I don't ever remember going back to the house again.*

*I find it interesting that these two stories both detail visits to "haunted houses." They could be emblematic of the images I'm haunted by, the memories that start me off on a story.*

*"Testament" was published under the name Kay Harris.*

## *Testament*

Published by *Cairn*, 2007

Every few months when I was a child, my family escaped from the crowded streets of inner-city Minneapolis and drove 200 miles north to the small town of Spruce Park where my aunt and uncle lived. My grandparents' cottage was in the wooded countryside nearby.

On this visit, Daddy drove our new car—a 1957 Chevrolet Impala—dark copper with a wave of corrugated aluminum trim on each of its stylish fins, and the whitest of gleaming white sidewalls. He said it was his last chance for pizzazz—at the rate we were going, the next car would be a station wagon.

The radio was tuned to comforting lyrics which included Mama's favorite—Perry Como. Every once in a while, when she was preoccupied with Annie, my father turned the knob, then peeked back at us with a devilish grin. Before you knew it, there would be the thumping rhythms of Elvis. It usually took my mother a few minutes before she realized what he had done, and flipped back to her "wholesome" station with a remark about something being "inappropriate."

Riding along in a brand-new car, I didn't even mind the switch because I felt raised to some higher level of worth. Unless some other family made a surprise purchase, we had the premier automobile in our parish.

\*\*\*

"Grandma is divorced! She used to be married to somebody else—not Grandpa!" My brother's words kept repeating in my mind.

Usually, I led our Saturday-morning treks through the woods because I was the oldest at ten years. Mama instructed me to watch out for the others. After David's sudden announcement, my stun landed me in the back of our procession, with Margaret, my six-year-old cousin.

My brother had forgotten those shocking words once he'd blurted them out. He and John, my eight-year-old cousin—David's cohort in age as well as gender—readily took charge, forging down the path cut into tall evergreens. It wasn't really a path, but tracks made by years of tires rolling from one spot to another through 40 acres of timber. The smaller Norway Pines, which we each scrutinized, bordered our trail. Grandpa had marked "the special one" with a red tag. At Christmastime, Daddy would chop that tree down and we'd bring it back to The Cities, tied atop our new car.

On these hikes, we journeyed single file into the wilderness, avoiding the middle hump where grasses were long and prickly and full of burrs. Margaret, because she was tiny, would squeeze into the track beside me.

Grandpa had told us to watch for the chosen tree, so stomping along, we played an "I Spy" game to see who'd first spot the red tag. The winner would get an, as yet, unrevealed reward!

I usually felt giddy being on my grandfather's property. After months cooped up with two other children in a small house set on a city lot barely big enough for a beat-up swing set, the thrill of land ownership, no matter how detached, made me feel proud and free. On this day, after my brother's revelation, my grandfather had suddenly become—not that. My grandmother had been married to someone else in the long-ago past. Someone I'd never known. A person my grandma, my aunt, and my mother whispered about, in addition to other forbidden topics, while sipping endless cups of coffee.

Stopping for a moment to help Margaret tie her shoe, I brooded over David's words. "Oh, I hear lots of stuff that way," he'd boasted, jamming his walking stick, which also served as a sword, into the tire track and making a pile of earth that messed its smoothness.

"What sort of stuff?" I'd questioned, still unable to believe what he'd already told me, and that he sat under the open window often, eavesdropping. I was certain he hadn't committed any mortal sins— yet. Still, I wondered if he remembered to examine his conscience, then claim this nasty behavior, along with all his other venial acts, in order to make a good confession.

"That's for me to know and you to find out," he'd crowed, giving John a shove, then zooming down the road, sword raised above his head, a make-believe shield in front of his chest.

I ran my fingers through the sides of my recently-cut straight brown hair, trying to make it wave into a perfect ducktail. "Are you coming along?" I asked Margaret, whose pale blue eyes barely showed through smudged corrective lenses. Her shoes were in order, but now she dawdled, attention captured by a hammering woodpecker. She placed grubby fingers in mine and we followed the boys.

Margaret was a little slow. For sure, John wasn't watching out for her, always shadowing David. Countless times, Aunt Liz had said, "Margaret needs a bit of remedial work. That's all." Margaret told me she spent every school afternoon with Sister Mary Ignatius doing the alphabet and trying to put together more words than "cat" and "dog." When our kid talk headed into out-of-the-ordinary topics, Margaret floated off in the clouds like a balloon from the county fair accidentally set free.

"Do you know what divorce means?" I tried anyway, stopping once more, this time to push her stringy blonde bangs into a cockeyed barrette.

"No, not 'zactly," she said, and I decided not to pursue the topic. I wasn't even that sure what it meant myself, except that Trudy Mueller's parents were divorced, and the other girls at recess said Mrs. Mueller was going to Hell if she married her boss at the Red Owl where she worked as a cashier. She'd be excommunicated and never allowed the blessed sacraments again. When she died, the flames of Hell would swallow her up. I didn't know if her boss was Catholic, so I wasn't sure what would happen to him, but I knew it would be horrible. All the girls pitied Trudy. First, a father who'd disappeared to some faraway place—maybe St. Paul, but probably a lot farther than that. Maybe even

Chicago. And now, here was her mother, who never came to Mass anymore, tempting eternal damnation in trade for a life of sin on earth. I wasn't certain what this sin consisted of, but knew that the penalty would be never-ending pain.

Up until this time, the only pain I'd known was a broken ankle when I'd jumped off a climber on the playground and landed crookedly. For a while, I thought I'd die from that hurt, but I didn't. The excruciating pain from unrepented sin had to make you want to die, even though you were already a goner—sizzling away, forever and ever.

I'd asked my mother about Trudy's mother and her fate, but she'd shushed me up, saying, "This is Anne Mueller's business, Teresa. Not ours."

When I'd pestered, asking what exactly Mrs. Mueller had done, Mama had said, "You'll know about that in good time." The end.

"But what about Trudy? She'll be alone in Heaven if her mother and father both burn in Hell." Trudy Mueller had never been a favorite of mine. Her infrequent snaggle-toothed sneer, frizzy orange hair, and premature skin bumps put me off before I even heard about her parents. Still, I wouldn't wish anyone, even my worst enemy, to be alone with all their family burnt to a crisp. Trudy was an only child, too. This was unheard of at Holy Rosary Elementary. She didn't even have a spying, cheating little brother like David for companionship, let alone the baby who constantly clung onto Mama's skirts.

As I trudged toward the two hooting boys with Margaret stopping every few yards to pick up a pinecone, give it a look, then toss it away, I watched David's obnoxious behavior. He'd poked John in the backside with his sword at least three times, and now waved it, hollering something about "I shall conquer," while they waited for us to catch up. His darker brown hair stuck out at every angle. With more cowlicks than even I had, he'd never achieve a ducktail. I licked my fingers and, once more, rubbed them over recalcitrant strands. Watching David's antics, I knew his appalling words had been forgotten once they'd passed his lips. He wasn't churning over the condemnation our grandparents faced. In an effort to find a way out for them, I desperately began sorting through family history as I knew it.

From somewhere, I recalled one of Mama's many mysterious remarks. "After Mother left The Cities..." At some time Grandma had lived near us. She must have dwelt there with this other unknown grandfather. He must have run away like Mr. Mueller.

On our weekend trips to Spruce Park, we stayed with Aunt Liz and Uncle Rafe. They had a big old tan stucco-covered house in town. I slept on the extra bed next to Margaret's. David slept in one of John's bunk beds. Mama and Daddy used the spare room surrounded by a sewing machine, an ironing board, and the baby.

Saturday, we spent with Grandma and Grandpa at their cottage. We ate lunch, always topped off with Grandma's thick, sweet blueberry sauce in green glass service-station dishes. Grandpa's jokes and stories kept us entertained when we weren't roaming through the woods.

"I spy! I spy!" Margaret fell to her knees and groped into the lower branches of a perfectly-shaped pine. Grandpa had placed the red tag at a level where she would be the one most likely to find it.

"Here's the tree," I hollered. "Margaret wins." The boys turned around, shook their heads in disgust, but conceded that Margaret, indeed, was the victor.

Continuing our trek, I began to think about the next day. On Sunday morning, we arose early, skipped breakfast, and headed off to Mass, stomachs rumbling. When we got home, Aunt Liz and Mama hurried into the kitchen, donning aprons as fast as they cast aside coats. Within minutes, bacon and eggs appeared on the dining room table. In the afternoon, we'd return from the swimming hole or sledding hill, depending upon the season, to a huge Sunday feast of pot roast or fried chicken. My grandparents came to town for that meal.

Once I'd asked my mother, "Why don't Grandma and Grandpa go to Mass with us?"

She'd quickly, now it seemed too quickly, answered, "They don't want to drive this far for church."

I'd assumed they fulfilled their obligation at some little chapel out in the country. All of a sudden, the truth dawned on me. Grandma and Grandpa didn't go to church!

I slowed down again and looked at the blueberry bushes laden with dark pearls of fruit. Slipping from my grasp, Margaret knelt, this time picking juicy morsels and stuffing them in her mouth. From around a curve in the road, I heard the boys' loud voices like banshees screeching at each other. Hidden among green leaves, the berries looked like rosary beads waiting for a recitation of Our Fathers and Hail Marys. If I prayed hard enough, could I save my grandparents? Later that day, I knew we would go for a walk with Grandma, buckets in hand, picking berries that she'd make into sauce.

Right then, I decided that each time I picked a berry I'd say "Our Father"—merely that, the beginning words. "Our Father." "Our Father." Then, back at the house sorting out the leaves and stems before the berries were washed, I'd send my petitions to Mary in the same way. "Hail Mary." "Hail Mary." With each pinched-fingered throwaway, I'd address her. When I returned home to the city, I would dedicate a whole Rosary every day for them. My plan was set. Surely all this effort would rescue my grandparents. Hadn't the Rosary turned back the Turkish fleet? Didn't Mary herself promise St. Dominic that the Rosary was powerful armor against the tortures of Hell?

"What's the hold-up?" David had circled back and stood, one hand on his hip, the other resting on his sword.

"Yeah, we're never going to get there," John echoed, gesturing to hurry, T-shirt crawling up his jiggling belly.

I grabbed Margaret and yanked her on track. "C'mon, the boys are getting restless."

Now that we'd found the tree, we were headed off to explore the recently-vacated Harrington house, despite my warnings of bad trouble if we got caught. David had said, "How are they going to find out? Unless one of us tells…"

The Harringtons had been Grandma and Grandpa's neighbors forever. Sadly, Mr. Harrington had died the year before in mid-winter.

Pausing while re-reading Grandma's letter conveying this news, Mama had said to Daddy, who was sitting next to her on the sofa, "Gruesome the way those people up north store bodies for burial in the spring."

"What would you do, dynamite through solidly-frozen ground in order to get the remains planted expeditiously?"

"Stop making fun of me." Mama had punched Daddy's arm, but not hard enough to hurt.

All that winter, at peculiar times like doing arithmetic homework, I'd look out through white eyelet ruffles of kitchen curtains, and check the naked branches on our one big tree, an apple, hoping to see the first robin. Then I'd know that poor Mr. Harrington would soon be properly laid to rest.

Not surprisingly, Mrs. Harrington had followed her husband in death early this particular summer. There'd been no delay for her send-off. Grandma's letter said she rested next to Leo at the county cemetery.

The old couple had been kind to us when we hiked a half-mile through the trees to their house. Mr. Harrington would bustle, pushing extra chairs around the table, a huge smile on his face. His white teeth sparkled in a tanned, crumpled old face. Excited, he'd click them over and over again like castanets with a life of their own.

Mrs. Harrington would fix a plate of sugar cookies and pour milk. Then they'd sit there, asking about our plans and dreams. The last time we'd seen them together, I said I wanted to be a teacher—but not a nun! David wanted to be a soldier—big surprise! John supposed he'd be a soldier, too. And Margaret said, "Someday, I'm gonna be a reader!" The Harringtons nodded to each other as we ate—making us feel important.

One cold day, before either of the Harringtons had died, Grandma and Mama had huddled by the stove darning socks. I heard Mama say, "It's a crying shame Edith and Leo never had any children of their own."

Grandma said, "Well, of course, you know they were past all of that when they married. Edith had a child from her first…"

"Isn't it wonderful how hospitable they are to our children?" Mama interrupted, glancing toward me. The burning wood crackled while I kept my eyes on one of Nancy Drew's adventures.

Later, I'd wondered about Grandma's unfinished statement, but decided that Edith Harrington must have had a stillbirth like Aunt Liz did that one time. We never talked about it, either. Not after the family Mass. The small white box was put in the ground with Father Colby's prayers, and that was that. Aunt Liz's fat stomach disappeared with nothing to show for it but a flat stone marker in the Littlest Angels section of the Catholic Cemetery.

Walking through the woods, coaxing Margaret to keep on the move, I recalled that reference to Mrs. Harrington's long-ago child and decided maybe it wasn't a stillbirth after all. Maybe Mrs. Harrington had been married before, too, with a living child and a runaway husband somewhere. That would mean she, too, was divorced. This whole road could be full of little houses tucked in the trees where people lived, made cookies and blueberry sauce, told jokes and stories, and—waited for their punishment.

As we approached the small white Harrington cottage, I really began questioning David's idea to hike this way. My thoughts of burning forever had given me the jitters. On previous visits we'd heard conversational voices, or Lawrence Welk's music from the record player, sifting through the screen door. When Mrs. Harrington lived here alone, we could hear that the weather report was on the radio. She'd been standing at the window by her sink. Seeing us, she threw both hands up, waving as if prayers were answered, then rushed into the yard for hugs.

This time, no sound came from the house, its heavy front door shut. David twisted and pulled on the knob, but it wouldn't budge. At every window, the shade met its ledge. We couldn't even find a crack to peer in. The back door, locked up tightly, too, made me want to run back to Grandma. And, the empty green-painted window boxes made me want to cry. Every spring, Mrs. Harrington filled them with pansies—little purple and gold faces that greeted our arrival, and saluted us as we went on our way. This year, the boxes were full of dry brown soil and a mess of old yellowed stems. Some of them still held smashed blossoms faded to the same dusty color.

On the side of the house, slanted double doors built into the ground hid the cellar. Despite my warnings to leave them alone, David pulled on a handle, creaking open the right door, and flopping it onto the lawn.

"We can get in here," he said excitedly, inspecting a wooden stairway sinking into the murkiness. Both boys marched down the steps, their heads disappearing into the gloom.

Cautiously we followed, Margaret's limp hand stuck to mine.

It was a cellar similar to the one at my grandparents' cottage, with the same damp, musty smell that made my throat feel like I'd been eating clay. Solidly-packed dirt walls held a few shelves. Matches, lanterns, and sealed jugs of water—storm supplies—sat on them.

"Hey! Look what I found," David yelled. It was a flashlight with a low, almost worn-out, beam. He aimed it into the corners, jerking tentative illuminations so rapidly that I could barely make out the shapes of covered piles.

Underneath the tarps must be snowshoes, maybe garden tools, I thought. Suddenly, I wondered about the Harringtons' graves. What if these piles actually contained the old couple's bodies?

"Teresa—Ohhhhhh Tereeeeeesa." I turned toward the voice. My brother held the flashlight under his chin, face scrunched in a grimace of terror. By the reflected light, I could see John's normally small eyes dominating his expression. He looked more terrified than I felt.

"C'mon, let's get out of here," I ordered, grabbing Margaret and nudging John, who startled as if returning from a trance.

"Yeah, let's go," he stammered, tripping over the first step.

"You're yellow bellies," David scoffed. "Fraidy cats—fraidy cats." Then, "Oh my Gawd—lookit this."

I grabbed John's shirttail, making him fall, and slowly turned around, bracing myself for something horrible. On a workbench along one wall, sitting as if someone had just removed them, a set of false teeth leered at us.

Seconds passed before I said, "GO, right now!" This time, I pulled John's arm, hoisting him off his knees.

Margaret moaned something about "My hand—squeezed—my hand," while I hauled her up the stairs.

The flashlight thunked to the earthen floor, and the next thing I knew, David shoved into us, forging ahead. We raced to the edge of the lawn where lilac bushes made a hedge, and there collapsed in relieved laughter.

"Teeth! Can you believe it? Teeth!" David held his head, pondering this great puzzle.

John rolled around on the ground, clutching his stomach. "Jeez—I almost—barfed up—my waffles." His round cheeks shone bright red as he struggled for a breath.

Margaret glared at me, accusation darkening her lens-covered eyes. "You hurt my hand!"

"I'm sorry, Sweetie. I didn't mean to. I was afraid."

"Well—all right."

I rubbed her narrow shoulders, glancing back at the house. A rectangular black hole gaped at me—the right cellar door still lay open, its mate neatly closed.

"David," I said, "you gotta shut the door. If we leave it like that, somebody'll know we were here."

"No way. I'm not goin' there again."

"Oh David, c'mon. You're the brave one."

"Yeah, but you're the oldest." He started to whistle on a blade of grass between his fingers.

Fine time for him to notice, I thought, but said, "Everybody wait right here." I knew David might bolt at any second.

Creeping toward the door, I quietly chanted, "It'll only take a minute. It's going to be fine. Please God...Holy Mary..."

The door proved much harder to close. I reached underneath with two hands and, after several tries, finally raised it perpendicular to the ground. Before it crashed shut, I dared to look into the cellar one last time. A ray of sunshine pierced the darkness, revealing those shining white teeth, clenched in a grin of farewell.

After that, we barreled back to our grandparents' house. Margaret kept whimpering about her "aching side," but I urged her on. I didn't want to lose sight of the boys. They'd waited to make sure I didn't get sucked into the hole, then took off running, their swords forgotten. In order to more easily drag Margaret along the path, I took the middle hump by her side, thorns attacking my bare legs.

Grandma and Mama and Aunt Liz milled around the kitchen, slicing bologna and Velveeta Cheese for sandwiches, and setting the table for lunch when we tumbled in the back door. They said their usual "Slow down" and "Go get washed up" and "We'll eat soon." Deep in their own conversation, they failed to notice our agitation. None of us uttered a word about our adventure. Not even Margaret. We knew the last place in the world that we belonged was the closed-up Harrington house.

After the blessing, as Grandma passed a platter of sandwiches to Grandpa, she did say, "Did you have fun on your hike?" We nodded our heads and waited for the food. She persisted, "Anything interesting happen?" We shook our heads, staring at our plates. Under the orange and yellow lattice-designed oilcloth, I stroked Margaret's hand, which now smelled of Ivory Soap. Grandma said, "My, we are quiet today." But, she forgot about it. The adults went on with the kind of conversation they had when Grandpa, Uncle Rafe, and Daddy ate with us, speaking about the price of gasoline and the lawnmower that needed repairs. By the time blueberry sauce showed up, they leaned back discussing whether we'd have an early winter. At meals with them, no women talk full of intimations to secrets piqued my interest.

After lunch and cleanup, we prepared to go picking berries. Before we left, Grandma noticed my battered legs. "Teresa, you must be more careful in the woods," she scolded, covering the scratches with iodine—blowing each time she dabbed to take the sting away. I gazed at her silver curls bowing over my wounds, and prayed she'd live forever.

Uncle Rafe and Daddy had already headed back to town to do their men business, when Margaret snuck up to Grandpa and whispered in his ear. He said, "Good, Margaret. That's very good," and tweaked her nose. Then, he announced, "Margaret here found the special tree." David and John groaned, but we women gave her a cheer as Grandpa dug in his pocket and took out a quarter.

He stayed at the house, rocking in his chair, reading his newspaper, and smoking his pipe. Later, when we returned to the cottage, after the pickings were tended to, Grandpa would be full of jokes and a new story. Before we left for town, he'd bring out the Chinese Checkers.

Despite the excitement of our hike, I remembered my grandparents' plight and conveyed petitions to the Father and Mary with each berry I picked, and later when I sorted my contribution. That night in bed, listening to Margaret's sleeping snuffles, I folded my hands over the blanket's ribbon edge to say full prayers—many times. I fell asleep, praying hard for the souls of my grandparents. I also sent postscripts for the well-being of the Harringtons, who I hoped waited in Purgatory due to someone's, maybe the lost child's, intercessions, instead of already sizzling in never-ending flames.

***

When I was back at home in Minneapolis, the memory of the cast-aside false teeth became less scary. Instead of a shudder, re-living that first jolt of surprise, I began to consider the teeth in a different way. I thought about the impermanence of the human body, and how people could be dead and buried, yet leave behind tokens of living that stayed hard and intact. Even something so personal as a set of smiling false teeth could rest in a closed-up cellar, never changing, waiting for inquisitive children to stumble upon them.

It wasn't long before a new baby, Matthew, joined our family. As he predicted, Daddy traded the Impala for a Ford station wagon. A while after that, within days of each other, Grandma and Grandpa died. There was a joint service, held in mid-summer at Lofgren's Funeral Parlor, and later that weekend, Mama and Aunt Liz sorted my grandparents' belongings. All the way back to Minneapolis, I heard clinks from a box of green glass service-station dishes and blueberry sauce in jars.

## *KAUAI*

*Kauai is my husband's and my favorite Hawaiian island. A year or so before this story was published we made a trip there. Many of the situations are based on observations I made and places we went. A condo we stayed at was above Hideaways Beach or Pali Ke Kua. Visiting this secluded beach was one of the many highlights of that trip. The steep, slippery trail down proved to be quite treacherous. The plot is from my imagination. I have thankfully never lost a child. Our son played basketball and years after he was on a select team in middle school I heard about another player who had died after a high school game. I don't remember that boy's name or know where he was at the time of his unexpected passing, but the idea of an event like this has stuck in my mind. The loss of a child is one of the most difficult challenges of a marriage. Putting myself in the place of that long-ago boy's mother brought about this story.*

# *Kauai*

Published by *Cadillac Cicatrix*, Spring 2009

By the time we pick up our luggage at the Lihue Airport and head for Avis, dusk has settled. Ben bolts ahead of me, carrying his suitcase in front of him with two hands. I tried to talk him into buying one with wheels on some happier trip, so he wouldn't aggravate his tennis elbow, but no, even though he's not that much bigger than I am, he lugs it himself. I drag mine along. It's eighty degrees, and there's a thick layer of humidity. Nine hours ago we left our house in Seattle.

"Carly, are you coming?" Ben turns and looks at me like I'm a dawdling toddler.

"I'm not as fast as you." Even when you're carrying your own.

The car, a red Mercedes convertible, picked out by Ben, takes another half hour to sign off on. By this time darkness surrounds us.

Ben stops at the first intersection. He can go straight ahead, turn right, or turn left. "Which way?" he says. "We're looking for 56."

"Straight ahead?"

Ben turns right, drives by the north side of the airport, gets to another stoplight, then says, "I guess it's back that way." He U-turns and heads for the main intersection.

Are U-turns legal here? That's all we need—to start out with a traffic ticket on this "second honeymoon" that Max, my father-in-law, insisted on giving us.

Ben turns right on a red light and goes north on 50.

I hope we're headed for the condo in Princeville that his parents recently purchased. Pam, my mother-in-law, told me, "A trip like this will be good for the two of you. It's been over a year since Dale... And it is your twentieth anniversary coming up." She couldn't bring herself to say "died."

I thought about our first honeymoon, spent here in Kauai at the Coco Palms. Max paid for that one, too. My parents in Elma, "The Slug Capital of the USA," couldn't have afforded such a gift, and, as college students, we sure didn't have the money. I didn't tell Pam, "I don't want to go to Kauai. I don't want a second honeymoon. I don't even know if I want to be with your son."

Instead, I shook my head in agreement, which I always do with his parents.

An hour later we're traveling along the same road, and signs now identify it as 56. Aren't we getting any closer? All I want is a bed—and sleep. Traffic is scarce, and there are no discernible buildings. As our headlights pierce through the gloom, my chest tightens with the rhythmic swoosh of waves. As tired as he is from countless late nights at the office, Ben might miss a curve, and the car could catapult over a cliff.

At last, I see another sign: Princeville 21 miles. "Still twenty-one miles!" My voice clangs in my ears.

"We've gone over twenty. Dad said it was twenty-five." Ben sounds like he's just played three sets.

Minutes later we reach Princeville's entrance, with its huge fountain and statue of Neptune. When we get to the Pua Poa complex, I yell, "There it is!"

He pulls past the guard house for the hotel, U-turns, and goes back to the condo parking lot, where we sit, staring at several looming, unlit buildings. "Which one do you think it is?" I say.

"The unit is 403. We'll have to go searching."

The entry areas are almost as dark as the road. We stumble along, tripping on a curb here, a tropical plant there. At our third try we find the right building. On the top landing we face two sets of double green copper doors. Faint illumination sifts through etched-glass inserts. Ben says, "We're to the left."

"How do we get in?"

"There's a lockbox." Ben runs his hand over the stucco wall. "Here it is." He takes a piece of paper from his pocket, holds it up to the skimpy light from the door, and says, "The code's two, three, three, one." After several tries, with no luck, he says, "What are we going to do?"

"Sack out in the car?"

Ben takes off his skinny, black-framed glasses, rubs his eyes, and puts them back on. With a couple more attempts, the box cover miraculously thunks onto the tile floor. Once he figures out which way to turn the key in the lock, he opens the doors to a huge expanse of room with one dimmed lamp in the far corner. Windows that reflect us looking like a pair of exhausted refugees fill the ocean side. The ceilings are at least fourteen feet high.

"This place could be a Hollywood set," I say, feeling a tug for my cozy office at home.

"Dad told me it was fantastic." Ben puts his hand lightly on my shoulder. I'm too tired to move away. "Let's go get the luggage and crash. We can appreciate it tomorrow."

Ben, carrying his suitcase, pants like an old black Lab as I thump mine up the many banks of stairs.

It's 11:00 p.m.

***

By 5:00 a.m. I'm awake, lying on my right side, curled up with my arms tightly wrapped around myself. Ben, who's still out for the count, lies too close. I scrunch to the edge of the bed. Rain like falling tears splatters glass panels of the solarium across from this room. I didn't expect to wake up to a downpour. What did I expect? Nothing. I have no expectations. Just a wish that someday Dale will reappear. He would have been up early, anxious to get to the beach.

Pam told me, "Hideaways or Pali Ke Kua is a real treat. It's treacherous getting down there, but it's private and fun to watch the surfers." She searched my face, then said, "Stick together and be careful."

Ben throws his arm across me. I crawl out from under his grasp and pad to the windows.

"Are you up already?" His voice is muffled.

"I can't stay in bed any longer—jet lag." I don't turn.

In this solarium is a chaise upholstered in palm tree design fabric. It looks comfortable enough to sleep on. Four floors below me is a small yard. If I walked out there, beyond the low black chain fence, which serves as a warning rather than an actual barrier, I could float over the bluff down to Hideaways.

"We can get breakfast. Dad said the Wake-up Café in Hanalei makes great omelets, and they open at six."

"Did he?"

I can feel him staring at my back, and when I don't answer: "Do you want to do that?"

"If you do."

I really want to stay at this window all the rest of the day, all the rest of the week, and when I get tired I want to lie on this chaise. Two young men walk along the path north of the condo with surfboards strapped to their backs. The rain has stopped, the sun is coming out, the sky is streaked with pink. It makes the boys' healthy, tanned bodies glow.

"So, we'll get ready?"

"Sure." I tear myself away from the boys' progress down the hillside.

***

Wake-Up Café is one small room with a narrow porch—the whole place no bigger than Dale's bedroom. On the walls are pictures of surfers, some from fifty years ago—many of them even younger than Dale.

While we wait to be seated, an old couple, probably mainlanders who retired to Kauai, stand ahead of us. There is a thin girl with dark hair pulled back in braids. She greets us with a big "Aloha!" Her purple-flowered wraparound dress swishes as she reaches for menus. Two hefty Hawaiian women cook up a storm in the tiny kitchen. I've seen this before—small, delicate young women, and after a few babies, they become obese. Maybe it's too much poi. I never lost all the weight after Dale was born. Not until this past year.

The girl says to the old couple, "You can sit down—I'll have your order right up."

Once tall but now stooped over to about five and a half feet (our height), the man looks from beneath scraggily eyebrows, and croaks, "Don't make our usual. We want something different."

His wife, half a head above him, says, "They're so fast around here, we have to tell them if we want something new, or they'll bring our regular order before we can even get sat down." She turns and grabs the old guy's arm, leaving behind a cloud of Jungle Gardenia as she helps him to their table.

I can't imagine us at that age.

Five minutes after we order our omelets, there they are, steaming. I stare at my heap of eggs and cheese and wish I hadn't let Ben talk me into such a large meal. He also got a macadamia nut cinnamon roll that the server said was terrific. I nibble at it. Before, I would have felt badly about leaving food. At Mom's table nothing was ever wasted. Fifteen minutes later we're finished, and I wonder what we're going to do with the rest of the day.

"I thought after a stop at Hanalei Lookout, we can drive to the end of the road. There's an eleven-mile hike—the Kalalau Trail. We could walk on it for a short ways."

His parents seemed to have completely filled Ben in—right down to correct names. "We'll see…"

The Hanalei River Valley looks exactly like the picture on a postcard Max sent when they came over to buy the condo. He wrote, "This is where the islands' taro grows. That plant they use to make poi. Pretty terrible. Try it once and judge for yourselves. You'll love the lookout."

Max was right about the scenery. The many shades of green in the quilt-patterned fields along each side of the winding river are as breathtaking as those we saw in Ireland during a trip Ben and Dale and I made when Dale was in sixth grade. Dale kept us in stitches with his accent and limericks. This is the first time we have gone anywhere without him. The apex of our triangle, he held us together. After his death, months blurred with the simplest acts of survival. As time has passed I feel the shape of our life pulling further apart, and I don't know if I care about remolding it.

Shortly before we get to the end of the road, Ben points out a pasture full of horses— mostly palominos. Just beyond, hikers take off on their trek along the inaccessible Nā Pali Coast.

"There's the first of the wet caves—Waikanaloa," he says.

Pulling into a parking place, we're so close, I can almost reach out and touch the freshwater pool. Quite a few cars maneuver through the tight area, and I wonder if any ever slip into the water. Dale, seeing the lidded-eye shape of the cave, would have said, "I'm snorkeling in there." If I jump in the water and swim for that dark opening, will I find him?

Ben says, "If you want, we can hike to the other wet cave— Waikapala'e—it's close. There's a Hawaiian legend that it was dug by the goddess Pele for her lover." He smiles invitingly.

"I'd rather go back and watch the horses."

Several are swaybacked, with ribs protruding. There's a pregnant mare and another one with a foal nursing. A robust-looking stallion stands watch over his herd with a white bird (Ben tells me it's an Egret) on his back. In spite of myself, I smile.

***

Another day, after another breakfast at the Wake-up Café, Ben says, "You sure didn't eat much."

"I wasn't that hungry."

"You haven't been hungry for months."

"If you really want to know, the sight of food makes me sick."

"Of course I want to know. You look like you've lost at least fifteen pounds."

"Isn't that good?" He used to say I was too heavy.

"You've always been fine for me. More than fine." He reaches out to take my hand. I let him hold it for a moment before pulling away.

As we head for the Mercedes, he stops and riffles through a rack of sundresses in front of a gift shop. "Would you like to buy one of these?"

"I brought enough clothes." In my wheeling suitcase.

"You might like something special from our trip."

"I don't think so."

Once we get on the road, he says, "We can go down to Port Allen and take a cruise along the Nā Pali Coast since we didn't do the hike. Does that sound like fun?"

"Sure."

As we drive south Ben says, "Look at all we missed coming up here in the dark." He slows and turns his head at the road sign, then laughs. "It says 2.1 miles, not 21 miles. That sure gave us a shock."

How stupid.

"Look at all these new buildings. None of this was here last time. They came after the hurricane in '92."

"I wonder how old-timers feel about the construction."

"Hate it. Have you ever heard of residents anywhere liking it when bigger, more expensive houses and condos come into their space? I'm sure it's helped the economy."

Spoken like a true Republican.

"I'm also sure they'd pull up the drawbridge and keep the builders, as well as the tourists, out if they could."

"You're probably right." We used to argue about this sort of thing—me spouting opinions in the same way I did with my logger father, who defended clear-cutting on the Olympic Peninsula.

"We could go visit the little town of Kīlauea and the lighthouse one day. Remember when we did that before? It was the farthest north we drove."

"Vaguely." I recall the white tower and a bluff covered with those same white birds as I saw by the horses. I felt dizzy looking down at the water. Ben blamed it on my pregnancy.

For several miles we're quiet. Then, as we approach Waimea, I see it. The Coco Palms. A battered, brown shell of the old Coco Palms. Totally deserted. Looking as if it could blow over at any moment. For the first time in months, I feel a pang about something other than Dale. "It's like a ghost town."

"You knew it was ruined in the hurricane."

"Yeah, but I thought it would be gone, bulldozed, not left here as a reminder of what it used to be. I don't understand why they would leave such an eyesore for all these years."

I picture our room with the conch sink and Jacuzzi big enough for two. I'd never seen such luxury. We took walks among the palms, listening to the call of a shell trumpet, watching torchbearers circling the area with their flames, seeing other people getting married or renewing their vows. It was here that we had many romantic nights, despite neither one of us wanting to be married and certainly not having a baby, despite Ben's wish for me to have an abortion, despite my refusal and my parents' wish to take me back into our Catholic home where four of my seven siblings still lived, despite his father's and mother's insistence that we marry and their explicit hope that this would make their only child settle down, get into law school, eventually join his father's practice. I wasn't their dream daughter-in-law. I wasn't Ben's dream wife. But despite everything, the magic of paradise took over, and our marriage began.

"They keep thinking someone will rebuild or transform it into condos." He gazes at the site of our honeymoon, seeing something different than I'm seeing. "If you want we can come back here and go through the old grounds. I heard they still have weddings among the palm trees."

"Would you really want to go in there? It looks like it should be condemned."

"Maybe next time it'll be restored to the old glory."

"Maybe so," I say but think, I don't ever want to come back here again.

***

Our cruise along the Nā Pali Coast in a catamaran that holds fifty is fine until we get to the turnaround. Choppy waters make several people seasick. Ben and I sit on a bench, port side, watching the cliffs. Gradually, the landscape turns into smaller hills and beaches. I feel nauseated and don't want any of the chicken teriyaki that most of the passengers line up for.

"You get a meal," I tell Ben.

"No, we can find something later."

"Thanks. The smell is making me feel awful."

One boy has spent most of the cruise on a gangplank, bouncing with the waves. He's tall, with a tattoo of some Asian sign on his arm, and looks like he could be a basketball player on Dale's team. I wish I would've let Dale get the tattoo he wanted. I imagine this kid on one gangplank, Dale on the other, hollering back and forth to each other. Now, this boy pays for his earlier exuberance—his complexion looks green. But he'll leave the catamaran and be back to normal in another hour. For the hundredth time I wonder if Dale's boundless enthusiasm was his downfall.

If I mention this Ben will say, "That's illogical. It would have happened no matter what. It's how his body was made." So, I don't tell him my thoughts. I quit voicing them months ago, around the time when he suggested a grief counselor "...to help you get through this."

"What about you; don't you need something to help?"

"It's the most horrible thing that has ever happened to me, but I have clients who need my attention. I have Dad's work to sort through." Eighteen months ago Ben convinced Max it was time to retire. He was in the process of reorganizing the firm when Dale died.

I was writing the second edition of a chemistry textbook and meeting with its publisher in Chicago the night Dale went to bed— never to get up. A blizzard hit, trapping me for forty-eight hours.

On one of many calls, Ben said, "The doctor feels it's essential to perform an autopsy immediately."

When I finally got home, Ben said, "You wouldn't have wanted to see him after that."

Dale had been cremated, and all I have left of my son is an urn full of ashes. They could be anyone's ashes.

Afterward, several times Ben suggested, "Don't you think work would give you something to take your mind off Dale?"

"I don't want to take my mind off my son!" I would answer.

I had a contract, but I bagged out on it. I couldn't concentrate on formulas. They offered me an extension, but I couldn't fathom ever going back to that book. Eventually, I started another one—a new grammar text for elementary school students. I can shut my office door and stay there from early morning, all through the night, catching a little sleep on my sofa.

Obviously worried about the state of our marriage, Max and Pam came up with this trip.

It's almost dark when the catamaran docks. The boy and his family walk ahead of us toward our cars. I hear his father say, "A bit much for you, huh, son?"

The boy takes off at a lope, a younger sister racing behind. I can picture her sympathizing with him, then insisting on a turn at his Game Boy.

"I don't want to drive this road again in the pitch-black. Would you mind a fast McDonald's instead of a decent meal?"

"Fine with me." Dale, like all his friends, used to love McDonald's, along with every other type of junk food. Could it have been the saturated fats? If I hadn't been so busy with my work, made more nutritious meals, more fruits and vegetables, would things have been different?

***

The next day Ben tells me that we're going to Na 'Āina Kai. It's two hundred forty acres of botanical garden and sculpture park.

"This is interesting," he says, reading a tour book Max sent along. "It was started by the ex-wife of Charles Schulz, you know, the guy who did Peanuts."

What would I do with my settlement if I were to become an ex-wife?

We arrive at the Orchid House and sign up for the Ka Waimakai Walk. The place is full of exactly the sort of people who would gravitate to this type of activity—well-off and middle-aged or older. The women are fully made up, in bright-colored designer resort wear. Their husbands are garbed in "roughing-it" costumes purchased from expensive sportswear companies. Max and Pam would fit right in. There is a pair, however, that doesn't look at all like they belong. They have to be in their twenties.

The guy wears a navy-blue polo shirt and rumpled cargo pants. It's the girl who I secretly scope in on. She has long, silky, brown hair cut to shoulder length, and golden, tan skin polished with some sort of sweet-smelling oil. She wears an iridescent-pink sundress with thin straps, a smocked bodice, and a skirt that hits just above her knees. The bottom of the skirt is sprinkled with sequins. Did her husband buy this dress for her from the outdoor rack in front of an island gift shop?

Standing under a vine-laden arbor, she would make a perfect model for a Na ʻĀina Kai brochure. They are the only others on our tour.

I feel old and frumpy in my gray T-shirt, gray pants, and gray jacket tied around my waist. I feel like the scrubber woman in some dingy apartment building. Ben—in his orange button-down, collared shirt and pressed jeans—is oblivious to how I'm feeling, and if he's conscious of the young woman, he's pretending not to be.

The leader, a portly fellow in a green jacket with the garden logo on it, wears knee-high socks that reach to almost the bottom of his walking shorts, along with laced boots. We all have on sandals. He says his name is Larry and that he lives in nearby Kīlauea. "Been there since the eighties." He's probably one of those who would hate all the development. In the past I would've grumbled with him about it.

Through the walk into the jungle, I lag behind, taking pictures with Ben's new digital camera, always conscious of the girl, trying to get her in a few shots to study later. I notice she isn't as thin as I had first thought.

Every few minutes Larry stops to tell us about some beautiful flora specimen, showing off his knowledge, giving us more information than we will ever remember, shrugging off all questions and comments. We obediently tag along.

Small flies start nibbling at our bare flesh. I put on my jacket and am protected. The girl gets the most attention. Where she stood quietly, pristine-looking, as we began our tour, by the time we are in dense foliage, she is pushing her hair off her face, rubbing at her arms, and bending to swat at her legs. The husband gives her little pats.

Larry shows us the fruit from a noni plant. "This white, pimply looking ball has a fetid smell like the worst cheese ever. It'll stay on your shoes for days. Be careful!" He pokes at a fallen glob with a stick and gives each of us a whiff. It is putrid. I have an urge to push the girl into a pile of it.

Upon reaching the beach and respite from the bugs, her husband asks Ben if he will take a picture of them together. He says, "We're expecting a baby in five months. This is our last vacation by ourselves," and puts an arm around his wife. She rests against him, obviously glad to be done with the ordeal of our hike.

I feel horrible for my nasty thoughts.

The young man offers to take a picture of us, and when he looks at the screen of Ben's camera, says, "This is great."

It is good. We look like twins with our similar fine-boned bodies and short, brown hair. If Dale were towering between us, this could be our next Christmas card.

*** 

We walk to the Princeville Hotel for a luau one evening and have our first taste of poi. I don't know how we were fortunate enough to miss it on the last visit.

Before singing and hula dancers start, our emcee, a robust Hawaiian woman with three white floral leis, welcomes children on stage to play while the drummers warm up. One little boy catches my eye. He is about eighteen months old, dressed in a shirt with a dolphin on it, shorts, red sandals, and a complimentary lei of tiny seashells. I sip a Mai Tai and watch him. On his head is a red baseball hat turned backward. What a character, cavorting and making faces.

In spite of our honeymoon in paradise, Ben was miserable during those months afterward, waiting for "the baby"—I'm sure remembering keggers with friends and thinking of all the things he would rather have been doing than working at a 7-Eleven or sitting in a cramped apartment with his pregnant wife. I sure felt that way as I stood with an aching back at the ironing board we'd picked up at a garage sale—pressing other people's clothes in order to earn a few extra dollars. We both were able to continue at the University of Washington, thanks to Max's generosity. Once Dale got here, we fell in love with his huge grin and infectious laughter.

This little guy onstage has those same qualities. His mother stands by the side, hands reaching toward him every time he gets too close to the edge. It was easy to save Dale from harm at this age. If only I had been able to reach out and hold him that night. Save him from his journey into darkness.

*** 

This morning, as usual, I'm awake before six. The sun streams in. On every other morning I stayed in the condo on the chaise, waiting to see what Ben had planned. Today I decide to explore Hideaways Beach by myself. Maybe surfer boys will be there before too long, and I can see them up close. Ben lies flat on his back, snoring. It'll be a couple of hours before he stirs. For a second I consider leaving him a note. But I don't want him to know where I am.

The steps are steep and staggered and built halfway down the slope into red clay. When I get to their end, I see a strip of path going straight for a drop-off, and then turning abruptly to the right, where it winds down at a less scary angle. Someone could slip before reaching this turn and fall onto the rocks and water below. Momentarily, I wish Ben was with me. Then I tell myself, You can make it. Sidestepping onto grass and working my way along, I'm pleased with my balance. Before long I'm on the beach, all by myself, with the roar of waves enveloping me. I sit on my towel and wait and watch, mesmerized by the continuous movement. A pair of surfers appear through the foliage. They nod at me and head to the far side of our cove, where they put up a small, blue domed tent. After leaving their belongings, with boards under their arms, they run for the water. One has a mop of curly, dark hair, just like Dale's. I watch them catch waves and, after a few seconds, fall. It's hard to get much of a ride here.

"The surfing is only for experts," Max said. "As far as swimming, look out for strong currents and sharp coral. Only go in when the water's calm." I hope both boys are skilled enough. Perhaps I should stay until others show up—make sure they're OK.

"How come you're down here all by yourself?" There stands Ben.

"I woke up. You were still asleep."

"You could have left a note."

"How'd you know where I was?"

"I always wake up when you leave our bed. I heard the door shut and watched from the balcony, got ready, and here I am." He plops down on his own towel. "That trail is sure steep and slippery."

"It wasn't that bad." Can't I have a few minutes to myself? "I wanted to be alone," I say. Then, when he looks at me with his eyebrows raised, "There's no reason for us to stay together, you know."

"What do you mean?"

"Without Dale, there's no reason for us to stay together."

He faces me for a moment, then picks up a small branch and starts drawing two stick figures in the sand—holding hands. "How 'bout if we enjoy the beach?" he says, ignoring my comment. "Let's go swimming."

"You know I don't like to swim in the ocean." The last time was with Ben and Dale on a Panama cruise a couple of years ago. Our ship stopped at a little island where we rented a cabana. After playing in the waves, we ate our lunch and watched Dale bodysurf for hours before he crashed on a lounge chair. When it was time to return, we had to shake him repeatedly before he awakened.

We had a good laugh about it. Was that a warning? Was it a foreshadowing of what was to come? A late-evening basketball practice, him getting home and heading straight for bed without even eating the dinner that Ben told me he had prepared. The next morning he wasn't able to rouse our son. What if I had been home? What if I had checked on him that night, the way I always checked on him before I went to sleep?

Ben runs into the ocean. A wave raises him high, then drops him. Water reaches to his waist. "Come on in," he hollers, gesturing with his hand. He lays back, staring up at the sky, letting his body lift and fall, appear and disappear.

I stand with water up to my ankles.

"If you come out this far, you can float here next to me." Ben's voice is almost inaudible.

I wait for a couple more waves. The water creeps up to my knees. What about the surfer boys? I need to pay attention to them.

"C'mon. I miss you out here, all by myself."

I take a tentative step, and another one, and many more. I'm up to my waist, and he's floating next to me.

"Lie back—let the waves take you."

I stand there, going up and down, ready to dig my toes into the sand and plow back to shore, race up that slippery path and as far away as I can go.

Ben takes my hand. His is hardly bigger than my own. "I'm here," he says.

He gently tugs me, and a wave comes, and I think, Why not just lie in the water and let it take me where it will?

I ease myself backward and start to roll. It's like a cradle. We used to have a cradle that we rocked Dale in when he was a tiny baby with colic. Now I remember—he wasn't always lively and cheerful.

The doctor said, "Some babies are so tightly wound, they need to blow off steam—use up energy in order to quiet themselves so they can rest."

His little body would stiffen in pain, and he would cry out each night, and after what seemed like hours, while one of us continued to rock the cradle, back and forth, back and forth, finally, he would drift off.

Perhaps this is how it felt for him, this leaning into the waves and letting go. Ben told me, "His face was peaceful. It must have been easy."

He gives my hand a little squeeze. "Are you alright?"

"This is nice…we could stay here forever."

"We can stay for a long while. And when it's time to go, we can still be together."

Right this minute, while the waves rock us, I think maybe this is what I want.

## THE RADIO

*When I was nineteen years old and married to a sailor during the Vietnam War, his first assignment was in Long Beach, California aboard a cargo ship. The apartment we lived in was very much like the one described in this story. For an inexperienced girl from Minneapolis this apartment building where I spent almost a year by myself gave me many images that stuck in my mind into my middle years when the story was written. Things like those described happened during those earlier years, but as with all fictional stories the events simmered in my imagination and eventually came out in a cohesive package. Most of the details are different from what "actually" happened. That's what is so much fun about writing fiction—the freedom to ask myself "What can I do with this idea to make it more interesting?" Even though I did live in a place like this, I would never call the story "memoir." Too many liberties have been taken during the writing.*

*Early readers continually asked me for more. This story was the jumping-off spot for my novel* Making It Work.

# *The Radio*

Published by *Lullwater Review*, April 2010

"Medio's the shortest street in Long Beach—only one block." That's what the Manager told Jimmy and Sheila Gallagher when they rented a furnished efficiency at Medio Apartments in June of 1966. The pink stucco building, circa WWII, had a couple of straggly palm trees in front, symmetrically planted on either side of an archway, that led to a raggedy-lawned patio. Each unit on the two floors had its own entrance door, like a motel back in Minnesota. Jimmy insisted on the second floor so Sheila would be safer during all her time alone. For the first several months that Sheila lived there, Jimmy spent few nights with her. Recently married, the young couple made good use of the apartment when they could be together.

A kitchen, a bathroom, and a sitting room with a Murphy bed that came out of the wall rented for $80 a month. Next door, on the bed wall side, lived an elderly couple who had retired to California from Kansas. They rented their apartment twenty years before because of its low cost and the short walk across Long Beach Boulevard to the ocean. The lady told Sheila that in the beginning they went every day. By the time Sheila knew them, it was a big event to haul out the walkers and totter over once a week. Mostly, they took in their sun on the flat, tarred roof of the building.

At night, with both beds down, Sheila listened through their thin, shared wall to the elderly couples' noises—snores and snuffles and trips to the bathroom and lots of rumbling, indistinguishable conversations. She imagined them discussing numerous aches and pains and memories.

On those times when Jimmy got leave from his ship, which seemed to be in and out on maneuvers nonstop, he laughed at Sheila as she insisted that they sleep with their heads at the foot of the bed "to get as far away from the Ancients as possible." He teased her for blasting the radio during lovemaking. "So they won't hear us."

"We hear enough from their side," he said. "Besides, maybe it'll bring back good times for them."

Unconvinced, Sheila insisted on the camouflaging rock and roll.

Mrs. Ancient once commented, "You sure play that radio a lot when your husband's home."

Sheila said, "He's a great music fan. Hope it doesn't bother you."

With a wry smile, the lady answered that it didn't.

The unit on the other side of Sheila's remained vacant, used for storage most of the time she lived on Medio Street. At least it stayed quiet. On their few dates to dinner and a movie, Jimmy and Sheila came back late, heady with the fragrance of night-blooming jasmine. Then, as they walked past the unoccupied apartment toward their own door, she would notice the Manager standing by his window at the other end of the building and say, "He gives me the creeps," as she watched him raise a bottle to his mouth.

"He's waiting," Jimmy would say.

And she would say, "I s'pose that's true."

To Sheila and Jimmy the Manager and his wife seemed old, but they probably were about fifty. Their apartment had a bedroom. In the bedroom the Manager's wife lay dying of cancer. The day the young couple rented their apartment, she had huddled on a rocking chair in the front room, fingers playing with a crocheted afghan—the skinniest woman they'd ever seen. They never saw her after that. According to the Ancients, he used to work at Douglas and she managed the building. After she got sick he stayed home taking care of her.

The Angel of Death never visited while Sheila lived on Medio Street—for either Mrs. Manager or for Mr. and Mrs. Ancient. But every time she heard a siren's howl, Sheila pictured stretchers and aid cars coming to cart one of them away.

Too soon the day that she dreaded dawned. They had been married less than six months. Sheila stood on the pier with a crowd of weepers. A band played "Anchors Aweigh" while Jimmy's ship left for Vietnam and Japan. The length of the cruise was unknown but Lifers said, "Plan for at least nine months." After the band dispersed and people drifted away, Sheila stood watching Jimmy's ship fade to a dot on the horizon, trying to keep him with her. She didn't worry much about him going to a war-torn country. After all, he was in the Navy. She mainly worried about the long separation and if he would remain true to her. She had heard lots of stories.

Once completely alone, Sheila's life became almost totally predictable: work all day, home and double-bolted in her apartment by 6:00 p.m.—no matter how high the temperature, no matter how many invitations from friends at the office to go out and experience Long Beach's nightlife. She holed up with her fan on, watching TV, wearing nothing but the T-shirt that still carried Jimmy's smell. Saturday, she bought a few groceries—mainly canned spaghetti and TV dinners, at the market near her apartment—and did a load of laundry at the room built into a corner of the sunroof. She always encountered the Ancients holding hands between lawn chairs under an umbrella, yakking away at each other.

Every payday Sheila shopped at a nearby department store, buying presents for Jimmy. Since she wasn't sure what he would like, she bought him stacks of Civvie shirts. She had also been told that when the sailors returned from cruises, they brought heaps of gifts—red-and-black enamel jewelry boxes, mother-of-pearl compacts, jade rings. Sheila wanted things to give back to him. She would place her accumulated purchases around her on the Murphy bed, turn the radio up, and imagine the celebration they would have when Jimmy finally came home.

Three-quarters through the cruise, his ship docked at Yokosuka. Husbands called their wives with news that the end was getting near. Sheila had been waiting for almost a week when the phone rang long after midnight. They stumbled through some words for a few minutes without much to say except how much they missed each other, which had already been said in letters. She teased him about the Yokosuka street girls, praying that he would stay away from them. He asked her about work and her friends there. Hearing his voice and knowing it would still be months until he returned, having nothing much to say and such a short time to say it in, this turned out to be the worst night of the cruise.

After the call ended with Jimmy saying, "There's a whole line of guys pushing for the phone," Sheila used the bathroom and went back to bed, where she cried herself to sleep. A short while later she awakened to water pouring on to the floor. The innards of the tank had gotten stuck, and the toilet gushed all over. Not knowing about the intricacies of plumbing, she made an emergency call to the Manager, who came rushing in to dam her flood. After he showed Sheila the knob that turned the water off, she sat on her chair, clutching her robe, knees under her chin like a chastened puppy. He had brought a mop and pail and rapidly sopped the water up, his robe swinging as he hurried to get it done before leakage seeped to the floor below.

When he turned to talk to her, his robe had parted, revealing his pitifulness, as he slurred, "Gotta get back to the wife. She's havin' a really bad time. Needs me to talk to her all night long."

Sheila learned about the functioning of toilets that night and about being so drunk from sadness that a person could not feel his own nakedness.

A few weeks before Jimmy came home, the Manager emptied the storage apartment next door, and new neighbors moved in. Sheila never saw them. He tended bar in San Pedro; she worked as his barmaid. Their hours were upside down from Sheila's.

For the first couple of nights, she didn't hear them. Then it started and, more nights than not, a repeat performance occurred. At 2:00 a.m. they arrived, slamming their door and speaking loudly. The clamor escalated. He hollered. She screamed. He accused her of coming on to customers—men she had spent too much time serving. She accused him of having a dirty mind. Before long Sheila would hear crashes against the wall, like chairs being thrown, and the man yelling, "Don't hit me, you slut!" The woman would shriek, "It's none of your business, you son of a bitch," and Sheila would hear another crash. The first time she had her hand on the receiver to call the Manager, when she heard,

"Sweet stuff—please stop," in the woman's softened voice. The noises changed. The man moaned, "Baby—oh, baby." For the next ten minutes, Sheila huddled in the dark, staring across the room at that shared wall (glad it wasn't the bed wall), waiting for their noisy release and wishing they had a radio on at peak volume.

The day, at last, arrived when Jimmy's ship came home. Sheila stood on the pier with the same crowd of wives and children, while a band played "America the Beautiful." Everyone stared at the hundreds of white uniforms in lines by the ship's railings. Eventually, Sheila recognized the face she searched for.

At 2:00 a.m. that night—spent and asleep—they jolted awake to the Bruisers' noises. Sheila hadn't wanted to concern Jimmy, so she had never mentioned the bartender and his barmaid.

"What the fuck—is he going to kill her?" Jimmy quickly ran through his options: call the Manager; call the cops; put on his pants and go save her himself.

"Just wait," Sheila assured him.

After it was over they cuddled on the bed listening to the snores and snuffles on one side and the complete silence on the other.

"They're probably sharing a smoke and rubbing new owies," Sheila said.

Jimmy said, "I guess that's one way to keep excitement in your marriage."

A short while later he got stationed on base. This meant that Jimmy would never have to leave again, so they moved to a bigger place.

The day Sheila returned their keys to the Manager, he told her, "Had to evict those neighbors of yours. Hope they didn't cause you too much trouble."

Sheila said that she had survived, and living next door to the elderly couple had been a delight.

"They've been married almost sixty years and still act like honeymooners." The Manager frowned. Sheila didn't think this quite the case, but maybe from his perspective. "Those others, the bar people," he continued, "fifteen years of wedded bliss, and somehow they haven't killed each other. It don't seem fair." Then, "You've been a good tenant. All the best to you and your fella."

Sheila thought about it and gave him a quick hug.

Being together forever and ever lasted two more years. Sheila wondered sometimes about Mr. and Mrs. Manager and how long she lived after they moved away. And she wondered about the Ancients, hoping when they finally went, it was together. And she wondered about the Bruisers and how many years their bodies held up.

Mostly, Sheila wondered about Jimmy and herself. It sure wasn't the way she had hoped. There never seemed to be a thing to talk about. Jimmy started going out at night with his friends from the base. Sheila started running with a group from the office. The new apartment turned into a mess. Nothing seemed to work—even the radio.

When it broke, they never bothered to replace it.

## SOUVENIRS

*My husband is a stockbroker or financial planner as they are now called, and over the years I have seen a lot of different personalities in this profession. Most of them have been quality people. There is no one in particular that I patterned Rich Plenny after; however, I also have seen some less-than-appealing people in this field and he is a composite of some of those male acquaintances. The rest of the characters are completely from my imagination as I tried to come up with a good plot. On one of our trips to Paris we visited the cemetery described in this story. It made quite an impression on me and I had to include it in some tale or other.*

*Whenever I travel to an interesting locale I try to come up with a story afterward. Sometimes this happens, sometimes not. The question I get asked most often about this story is, "What happens next?" Someday I might feel inclined toward re-visiting Shelley Piper-Plenny's life journey.*

# *Souvenirs*

Published by *TalonMag*, August 2010

Edrich Plenny yawned and rubbed his belly. "Sure could use a rest and something to eat." It was Monday morning in Paris.

What does he have to yawn or be hungry about? Shelley Piper-Plenny felt fine. There'd been lots of food and wine, as well as halfway decent sleep during the twelve hours since they left Denver.

"Rich Plenny" the guys at the office had dubbed her husband. When introduced to someone in this way, he always responded with, "It's never enough!"

Shelley called him Ed.

After upgrading the couple's economy class tickets to first class, he told her, "Skinny as you are, survival in steerage'd be easy. I need more room. Besides, Max and Dave are going in style." Whatever Max Berman did, Ed tagged along. And why wouldn't Dave Meyer spring for the extra cost? According to Ed, "He has more money than God, or at least Meredith does."

Max had reserved a Mercedes van. With so many pieces of luggage, he said, "Do you think one vehicle will be enough?"

The driver, a turbaned, dark-skinned man, apparently used to the situation, stacked and turned and shifted, while four of the travelers piled inside.

Outside, Max hulked over him. "Shove that one to the side." Ed stood behind Max, nodding. The driver ignored them both, and once everything, including Max and Ed, was stashed, he pulled the van into a line of traffic, heading to a boutique hotel on the Left Bank where Trinkler Investments had rented rooms for the week that their super achiever brokers planned to be in Paris.

Trinkler opted to proceed with their awards trip, April of 1988, in spite of Black Monday the previous October. After that scare, the Market, with a few blips, moved upward. Yet, a good deal of fear on the part of most investors still remained. Shelley nervously watched Ed's relieved conspicuous consumption. She'd done clerical work for ten years at Trinkler in the '60s and '70s, and couldn't help but recall an adage that most stockbrokers spend $1.25 for every $1.00 earned. Since his renewal of confidence, Ed constantly told her, "Loosen up. You don't have to be so damned cautious." Anxiety over losing her Cherry Hills dream house, with its numerous built-in bookshelves, and the crystal shop she'd owned for several years often set Shelley a-jitter.

Looking from her window behind the driver, she felt disappointed in the dirty-looking apartment buildings jammed close to the highway. Graffiti covered grimy walls. This didn't look like any Paris Ruth Perkins, her manager at the shop, had so vividly described, adding, "Go have an adventure to tell me about."

Leaning forward, Shelley said, "Who lives here?"

In Middle Eastern-accented English, the driver said, "Immigrants."

Once inside the city, it started to look right. While he circled and turned back onto Boulevard Saint-Germain (running up the tab according to Max) Shelley saw Notre Dame across the river. Eventually, he found a short street twisting away from the Seine, and at the end of the street Hôtel la Geste, a white stucco building with lacy black railings on balconies decked out with red tulips.

The clerk with a pencil-thin mustache drooping into his jowls sat at a Louis XVI-style desk. Visibly perturbed by their ruckus, he looked as if they'd brought in the stench of something spoiled.

Dave asked, adding a bit of sketchy French, if they could check in early. He looked pale and exhausted with his comb-over lopped to one side.

The clerk informed them, in perfect English, that the rooms would not be available until at least 2:00 p.m. "Your bags," he scanned the mass, "will be safe in our storage room."

Max, backed up by his scowling buddy 'Rich,' said, "We're with Trinkler, doesn't that mean something?"

The clerk shrugged.

Shelley noticed another man, an American, who wanted to check in early, too. This fellow, with an impassive expression on his tanned face, said in a calm voice, "D'accord, Girard. Be back in a few hours."

As he walked toward the double front doors, Shelley studied his tall figure in a dark blue crewneck sweater and khakis. Did his thick, grayish-blond hair need to be trimmed weekly in order to keep its casually mussed appearance?

Minutes later, the six Trinklerites traipsed down cobbled streets and settled on Le Petit Chatelet, a restaurant close to Shakespeare and Company. They were informed by a tiny blond woman, standing tall and using hand gestures, that it would be over an hour before any establishment started serving.

"What do we do now?" Ed sulked.

"That shouldn't be difficult." Louise Berman's recently operated-upon face remained stationary despite her tone. "We can go over that bridge and check out the cathedral."

Shelley had read about Sylvia Beach and the store with English books opened in the 1920s for expatriates. "I'd like to browse here for a while." She pointed at the gold façade with black writing. A hand-lettered sign in the window said, Be not inhospitable to strangers lest they be angels in disguise.

The men decided to walk back to a park called Viviani. "We can rest there and wait for you ladies," Dave said.

In the jammed shop, Shelley found a souvenir—an old copy of Les Misérables.

"Haven't you read that before?" Meredith Meyer spent so much time running and working out that she never read anything but the Rocky Mountain News.

"Years ago—a library copy. This'll be my own."

Louise attempted a face rumple. "Why would anyone want to read a book more than once?"

"Don't you think it's time to get going?" Meredith said. "After that plane ride and taxi odyssey, I could use some power walking."

Shelley decided to return to the book shop alone, after breaking free from the others, especially Max and 'Rich.'

At the office, Max, who was quite a bit older as well as more successful, and Ed (who was thirty-nine) shared investment ideas. Ed called Max "a self-made man. A real inspiration." Growing up the only child of the only single mother in Chambers, Minnesota, a town of 1,500, Edrich had been told, by his mother, that his name meant "rich and powerful." Trying to live up to it, he sought all the inspiration he could come by.

"Let's go find the darlings," Louise said. "Do you remember which way to go?"

"Follow me." Meredith strode forward.

The wives entered a low, metal gate to an impeccably maintained grassy area with pathways encircling a fountain. The husbands sprawled on a bench, dozing.

"They look like a trio of mutts in the sunshine," Meredith said.

"I figured they'd be watching pretty French girls go by," Louise said.

"This perfect weather would make anyone relaxed and drowsy." Shelley tried to shake off rumors about Max and his pretty assistant. Her warmed cheeks pinkened and a rustling breeze tap-tap-tapped like cotton balls. Even with the sophisticated women dressed in black, heels rapidly clicking as they passed by, an aroma in the air reminded her of church pancake breakfasts.

After an hour at the cathedral, which Ed described as "dark and dank and dirty," they raced like a herd of cattle heading for the barn toward Le Petit Chatelet. Halfway across the bridge, Shelley told Ed, "Save a spot for me. I want to stay here and take a few more photos."

"Don't be long. I'm ready for food and a nap."

She stood by herself, gazing at the Seine with its stone walls and walkways and strolling couples, wondering which bridge Inspector Javert jumped from. Here she was in the most romantic city. There wouldn't be much romance, if any, on this trip—certainly not like earlier days when Ed had preferred her company to anyone else's. He'd fall into bed every night, totally wiped out from food and wine, moaning about heartburn. Still, the city couldn't help but be romantic. She imagined events that had transpired here, soaked up the architecture, listened to the most elegant language. Even though she would have liked to turn and run the other way, toward Sainte-Chapelle, Shelley answered a tug and headed toward the others.

A young girl in jeans approached her. In barely recognizable English, she said, "This ring? Belong to you?" On her palm lay a wide gold wedding band.

"It's not mine."

"Worth much. Look." Something engraved inside seemed to note the amount of gold. "What do I do?" She raised unplucked eyebrows.

"Keep it. You won't be able to identify the owner."

"You take. A gift. Good luck." The girl handed the ring to Shelley, who pushed it away.

"No. Sell it."

"You have," the girl implored. "Maybe, please, something for my meal?"

She did look hungry and her jeans were raggedy. Shelley dug fifty francs out of her money belt. "This is all I can spare."

"Merci," the girl called over her shoulder, hurrying toward Île de la Cité.

Shelley rushed to the Left Bank, where Ed and friends sat at a table with a view of the river. They were all talking at once, and didn't immediately notice her.

At a pause, Ed put his glass of white wine down, glancing her way. "What took you so long?"

"A girl on the bridge. She found a ring." Shelley held the band out.

"You fell for that?" He rolled his eyes.

"What do you mean?"

"Didn't you read the warnings Trinkler sent?"

"No."

"She's a gypsy," Dave said.

"You should've figured that out." Ed seemed to expand.

Shelley picked up the glass of wine that Max had poured, feeling the ring grow hot in her clenched fist.

"Let's forget about it, huh?" Meredith said.

"Yeah. Okay. How much did you give her?"

"Fifty francs."

"Fifty francs for a hunk of brass! Remember this the next time you go off by yourself."

"Let Shelley look at the menu," Louise said.

"Sure. Hurry. The waitress'll be back any minute."

They all requested the plat du jour—veal served with a béchamel sauce, au gratin potatoes, and asparagus. Ed finished most of Shelley's.

On their way back to the hotel, he grabbed her hand, lagging behind. "Mad at me?"

"Not in the least."

"You were so quiet at lunch."

"Everyone else did enough talking."

"You are mad."

"What do you think? First you act like a jerk about the ring—make me feel the fool—then, I don't know, your whole attitude when Max is around."

"I didn't mean to hurt your feelings. C'mon, give me a little smile. We're in Paris—the place you've wanted to visit forever."

Shelley forced her lips to turn up.

"Let's go. We'll get in the room right away and take a nap before dinner. That'll raise your spirits."

\*\*\*

The brokers attended meetings several days until after lunch. Meanwhile, Trinkler provided activities for their guests. Louise and Meredith sputtered, taken aback, when Shelley told them she was striking out on her own, rather than going on a tour of Champs-Elysées and the Arc de Triomphe. Ed warned, "Don't get ripped off."

She made a beeline for the bookstore, feeling wonderfully unencumbered, but once inside, without the buffer of companions, awkward in her pale blue sweater and skirt. Other patrons, mostly dressed in jeans and carrying backpacks, leafed through books and mingled easily. Shelley twisted the brass ring on her thumb.

"Why don't you throw that away?" Ed had asked. "It's not worth a penny."

Shelley would keep it forever, as a reminder of a one-of-a-kind experience—another souvenir. Studying the copy of Les Misérables, trying to look absorbed, a clean, citrus fragrance on someone nearby caught her attention.

"I saw you at the hotel," the man from the lobby said.

"You tried to check in early, too."

"Have you been to this shop before?"

"Briefly."

"Lots of character." He ran a hand through his thick hair.

"I wonder about the living quarters. Where all those famous people stayed. Hemingway...Joyce."

"They were at the original. It was rebuilt here in the fifties."

"I didn't know that."

"These sleeping arrangements are small and low and cramped."

"You've stayed here?"

"When I was wandering through Europe, scribbling on what was to be my Great American Novel."

"You're a writer?"

"I used to fancy myself as one, before the real world set in and I had to make a living since no one clamored for my words. The written ones anyhow."

"That's sad."

"I still do write a story now and then. Never finished the novel. Do you write?"

"No. I'm just a reader."

"That's enough. Too many people think they have all these profound ideas to leave to the world." He looked pensive, maybe recalling his own efforts.

Customers pushed from all sides, trying to get to the shelf where they had been standing. "I need to pay for this book," Shelley said.

"Enjoy Paris." The man walked out the door with a small bag in his hand. He had made his purchase earlier and come back to chat with her. Shelley smiled picturing Ruth's probable reaction.

The next day, Shelley accompanied Louise and Meredith to Place des Vosges, with its upscale shops. Louise looked for cosmetics, Meredith for sportswear. The Victor Hugo House was on this square, and Shelley slipped away to it at her first opportunity. Neither woman showed any desire to join her.

While looking at the red embossed wallpaper and the four-poster made of dark wood, the bed where Hugo had last been alive, Shelley felt a tap on her shoulder. There stood the man from her hotel. "How's it feel to be in his house?" he said in that tranquil voice.

"Wonderful. This is where much of Les Misérables was written."

"Your friends aren't interested in France's greatest writer?"

"Not at all. I'd rather come alone than drag someone along who really doesn't want to be with me."

"I'm alone, too."

"I better be going. The others will be waiting."

"No time for an espresso?"

Why not? She could be friendly to this stranger. "Maybe just a few minutes."

"I'm Jeff Colmar from San Francisco." He held out his hand and she brushed her fingers across his.

"I'm She…Michelle Piper, from Denver. By way of a farm in Minnesota."

"Ah, Minn-e-so-ta," he said with a Scandinavian accent like the majority of people who heard of her origins.

"Not like that. I'm Irish."

"My people came from a town in the Alsace."

At a café's sidewalk table, Jeff said, "What brings you to Paris, Michelle?"

"A business trip for my husband. The company takes several employees somewhere every year."

"An awards trip."

"Right."

"He's successful at what he does." Now, he sounded mischievous.

"He's a stockbroker, and yes, I guess you could say he's successful. Not as successful as he wants to be, but working on it."

"What firm's he with?"

"Trinkler Investments—it's small."

"I know of them. Great reputation. My grandfather started a brokerage in the Bay Area. My father and brother are still part of it. They're always trying to get me to leave radio and join them."

"Radio?"

"I manage a local station."

"Sounds like a lot more fun."

"A lot less money, but I get by."

She wondered if he was married.

"It pays the bills for my wife and kids."

"Why didn't they come with you?" She couldn't help but ask.

"The kids are in school and my wife doesn't travel."

Was there a note of sadness? "How come?"

"She has lupus."

"A friend of my mother's had that when I was growing up. Very debilitating back in those days."

"It still is. Donna stays close to home."

"How many children do you have?"

"A boy and a girl."

"The perfect family."

"Yeah—before Donna got sick. I could bore you with details about that, and the problems of teenagers, but this is too nice a day. We're in Paris. I'm with a beautiful woman who looks like Jean...I can't remember her name."

"I don't know who you mean." No one had compared her to Jean Shrimpton in years.

"Such a pretty face. An innocence about her. Big blue eyes—like a child's." He sipped his espresso and looked at her with his own crinkly blues. "Do you have kids?"

"No." Then, uncharacteristically, "We couldn't have any, and my husband never wanted to adopt."

"Why not?"

"Too risky." These words felt disloyal, but it also felt good to say them. "He reasoned that everything was going well in our life, why take a chance?"

"After the last few years, I can understand his feelings. I'm hoping mine will learn to appreciate dear old Dad sometime soon."

"What about Mom?"

"They're loving to her, and don't like it when I travel."

"Does she mind?" Was this getting too personal?

"She understands. Matt and Kristy feel that Donna wouldn't be as sick if I stayed with her every minute of the day, but things could go on like this for a long time. She wants me to have my own life. Sometimes I take a trip for pleasure."

"Have you been to Paris often?" Safer subject.

"Many times."

"I've always wanted to come here, and so far, despite some mishaps, it's been beyond my expectations."

"What mishaps?"

Shelley told Jeff about the gypsy and showed the ring on her thumb.

"You haven't traveled to Europe without at least one encounter like that. It won't happen again. What else?"

For a moment she thought he was going to cover her hand with his. Shelley picked up her espresso. "Besides the wine and food, my husband isn't enjoying himself. He grumbled about being hot all through L'Orangerie yesterday, and he's making plans for his return to the office—calls his assistant every day."

"Not very happy with him, huh?"

"I'm not. I should be grateful. It's because of him that I'm even here. But yes, I'm annoyed as can be."

"You'll get over it."

"I suppose."

Shelley turned her attention to the plaza. Children kicked a soccer ball. Mothers sat on benches watching toddlers running and tumbling. Lovers lay on the lawn, oblivious to anyone but each other. Wistful music of a nearby violinist embraced it all.

She never complained about Ed, except to Ruth, her best friend as well as her partner in Piper's Crystal. Ruth never said so, but Shelley could tell that she thought Ed had a lot of less-than-desirable behaviors (the drinking, the overeating, their pallid sex life), but as Ruth often said, "He's a great provider," pointing to Shelley's personal collection of Baccarat and Lalique. Ed had set Shelley up in this shop as a consolation prize when she couldn't have a baby.

Ruth, after a messy divorce, had sworn off marriage. Instead, she carried on a string of relationships that lasted six months, tops. Once in a while she said, "If you ever want to meet someone…"

When Jeff Colmar suggested that they get together for an outing the next morning, "…if you're not busy with your friends," Shelley immediately reacted with, what would Ed think? Still, she asked, "Where do you have in mind?"

"Père-Lachaise. Do you know what that is?"

"Sorry, I don't."

"It's the largest cemetery in Paris, not far from here. Full of famous people, but it's not high on the hit parade of must-see spots. I'm sure your friends would never think of it."

"Sounds interesting." Beats shopping.

For the remainder of this day, which included a visit to Musée d'Orsay once the brokers were released from their mandatory meeting, Shelley's mind kept slipping to the upcoming time with Jeff Colmar. She decided not to mention it to Ed. She never questioned him about any of the lunches he had with women clients, and there was that time when a woman answered the phone in his room on a Scottsdale trip. She had accepted his explanation that, due to weight gain, he felt more comfortable getting a massage on a portable table in his room.

***

On Thursday morning, waiting in the hotel lobby, Shelley's breath kept getting caught in her throat. And then, there he was walking toward her, holding out his hand. Firm, quick, and matter-of-fact, their touch happened so rapidly that if she trembled, he couldn't have noticed. "Good to see you on this lovely morning."

She could back out right now, make an excuse, run for the tiny elevator. But, Ruth had told her, "Go to Paris. Do something exciting."

Jeff took her elbow and they walked toward the St. Michel train stop. "When do you have to be back?"

"My husband will be in a meeting until mid-afternoon."

"What did he say about visiting a famous Parisian cemetery?"

"I didn't tell him."

"Oh, I see."

They walked into Père-Lachaise at the Porte Gambetta gate. "This is a good way to enter," Jeff said. "Less overwhelming. Porte des Amandiers makes people claustrophobic, the tombs are so close to the path. Colette's grave is over that way. We'll see it when we leave." They walked up Avenue des Combattants past war memorials, and crossed Avenue Transversale No. 3.

"I didn't know cemeteries had walkways named like streets."

"As big as this place is, there has to be some way to find who you're looking for."

Several tourists, with open maps and dangling cameras, gestured this way and that.

"What's over there?" Shelley nodded toward a building with a dome, gilded flame, and chimneys.

"The crematorium." Jeff carried his own tattered map, but wasn't looking at it.

She had never known anyone to be cremated. All her dead relatives were buried in St. Raphael's churchyard back home in Minnesota.

"Those cubicles hold ashes." Artificial flowers decorated several of them.

"Maria Callas has a spot."

"She died brokenhearted over Onassis."

"That's the story. Let's go back this way." Jeff guided her onto Avenue Carette and soon they arrived at a stone tomb with an art-deco angel hovering. "Here lies Oscar Wilde."

"What are all those red marks?"

"Homosexuals have given their love. Did you know he became a Catholic before he died?"

"I didn't." Shelley recalled a photograph showing Wilde with foppish dark hair and dandified dress. "I like 'The Picture of Dorian Gray.' Such a strangely appealing story—to never grow old."

"I like his humor."

At Edith Piaf's, Shelley said, "The Little Sparrow." A large crucifix lay across the dark marble slab that covered her body.

"With an enormous voice. 'La Vie en Rose'—utter happiness when the war finally ended. She didn't have any regrets as she sang so well."

Would Shelley feel regret at the end of her life?

"See that bored guard?" A bedraggled, uniformed man flipped an idle finger toward a grave. "This is the most visited site. Kind of a fluke. Jim Morrison got in, when he died at twenty-seven, because his friends told the cemetery director he was a poet."

"Not one of my favorites, but I liked 'Light My Fire.'"

Wilted flowers and scribbled notes and an empty Jack Daniel's bottle littered the grave. How would it be to live so precariously?

Jeff said, "Wait'll you see what's next," and took her hand, leading Shelley through a convoluted path and stairways, with flat markers on either side. She'd all but forgotten what each stone covered. It seemed more like a scavenger hunt with this fun, interesting person showing her the way.

The white marble crypt, surrounded with potted primroses, had a statue on top of a bowing woman holding a lyre and a carved relief on the front depicting Frédéric Chopin. Burning candles flickered by the wrought-iron railing.

"We've now moved on to the sublime. His heart is in Poland, embedded in a church column. His music, such infinite beauty."

Others came and went while Shelley and Jeff, still holding hands, stared at Chopin's sensitive features. Too soon, Jeff said, "There's one other spot I want to visit before we leave."

"I don't want to see anything else after this."

"You will." He pulled her along to Avenue Casimir Perier. On the left stood a chapel-like structure with a cross. Beneath the canopied roof, two stone figures lay side by side.

"Who are they?"

"Heloise and Abelard."

"I've heard of them, but…"

"You said you're Catholic. They have an interesting place in our Church's history, besides being the oldest residents here."

"What happened?"

"Over a thousand years ago, he was a scholar and she was his much younger student. They secretly married and had a son. When her uncle, a powerful clergyman at Notre Dame, discovered their union, he sent a band of men to Abelard's bedroom in the middle of the night— they castrated him."

"Where was Heloise?"

"I don't know. He went to a monastery. She went to a convent. They wrote letters for twenty years. See the little dog at their feet?"

"I do."

"He represents their fidelity to each other. Finally in death, they're together."

"That's a very romantic story."

"This cemetery is one of the most romantic places in Paris. Many stories have ended here."

Jeff took Shelley to lunch after a short stop at Colette's grave on the way out of Père-Lachaise. Each had a crepe and a glass of white wine. On the wall of the café, a huge mural of Jim Morrison watched over the room. Memorabilia from other famous residents filled the place. Heloise and Abelard were not represented. When Shelley commented on this, Jeff said, "I guess a lot of people don't appreciate them like I do." And, with a crooked smile, "But, Jim Morrison. For the Americans!"

Shelley would have liked to hear more about the cemetery. Maybe someday if they were alone, without young people in jeans slurping onion soup at the next table, they could relive their visit.

Approaching Hôtel la Geste, Shelley said, "What about Victor Hugo?"

"He's in a tomb at the Pantheon. We could go there tomorrow morning. This is probably a spot you won't see with…"

"I'd love to. That's the last day of meetings. Then Versailles on Saturday, Monet's Garden on Sunday, and home."

Jeff ran a finger over Shelley's cheek. "Why don't you come down to my room—305—around nine. You can use the stairs."

"I will." What would a visit to his room mean?

They walked into the hotel like any other people who had met at the entrance door. By the elevator, Shelley saw Meredith Meyer, sweaty from a run and chugging a bottle of water. "Can I fit?" she asked, looking curiously at Jeff.

"You two ladies go ahead."

After the door closed, Meredith said, "Wow! Who was that?"

"I don't know." Shelley silently cursed her presence.

With a white towel wrapped crookedly around his belly, Ed stumbled out of the bathroom as Shelley entered room 432.

"What's going on?"

"I don't feel well," he said, gratingly. "Took a shower."

"Are you sick?" From all the wine and food?

"Upset stomach. Bad lunch."

"Where'd you go?"

"That place around the corner—the Hippopotamus. Had vegetable soup with a weird spice. Do I have a temp?" He leaned down so she could touch his forehead.

"You are warm. Do you want me to find some medicine?"

"I picked up something like Alka-Seltzer at a drugstore...a pharmacie." He put on a robe and began pacing. "I have to tell you something."

Lying on the bed, ready to lose herself in Les Misérables, Shelley waited. Ed appeared to be more than sick. He had a concerned expression like she hadn't seen since the evening of Black Monday. "What's wrong?"

"You know my money clip?"

"Yes." A sterling silver bull for a Bull Market.

"Someone swiped it."

"Stole it?"

"That's what 'swipe' means."

"How?"

"It was in my back pocket. I got jostled in a crowd. When I went in the drugstore, I right away noticed it was gone."

Shelley had told him that the clip made a big lump. Ed insisted it would be fine. "How much did you have?"

"I don't know. A couple thou…"

"Thousands of dollars!"

"At least I have all the francs and my wallet and passport."

"Would you please wear one of these belts under your shirt?"

Ed had said that no way would he put on such an uncomfortable gizmo, even though the company warned something exactly like this could happen. "Before I go out again."

"Are you feeling up for that?"

"I feel like shit."

"Why don't you rest and start over tomorrow?"

"I wish there was something on the tube."

"There are—lots of things."

"All in French."

When she left their room to join the Bermans and the Meyers for a walk through the Tuileries and dinner, Ed said in a muffled voice, from beneath the white duvet cover, "About that gypsy. I guess it's pretty easy to get taken advantage of in gay Paree."

"We'll have to be more careful." Shelley quietly shut the door behind her.

***

The next morning—Friday—Ed was too sick to get out of bed. "I'm here 'til I feel better. And, Shel, I'm sorry, I've acted like an ass this whole trip. It's just that Max… I'll make it up to you when we get home."

Will he buy me a piece of crystal or a first edition? "I'll be back later this afternoon."

"Where you going?" He might as well have said, Aren't you staying with me?

"There's so much to do. Carnavalet, the Picasso, the Opera House." Jeff had mentioned seeing Chagall's ceiling after visiting Victor Hugo. Would they even leave his room?

"Lots of those kind of places." Ed had complained of aching legs and feet during Trinkler's tour of the Louvre.

"I won't be back for lunch. They have room service."

He groaned unintelligibly.

At room 305, she tapped gently. No answer. She tapped again, a little louder. Still no answer. A maid came out of a supply closet and walked toward Jeff's door with a key. "No one here."

"Mr. Colmar is gone?" How could this be?

"Departed. Early today."

"I see." She didn't see. Where was he? How could he do this to her? No. There must be some logical explanation. These words competed in her head as Shelley stumbled the rest of the way down a stairway to the lobby—alternately angry and concerned. A cup of coffee. That's what she needed. She'd go to the cellar breakfast room and get her bearings.

"Madame Plenny, uh…Piper?"

Shelley turned.

"M. Colmar left this for you." Girard wore a smirk beneath his mustache as he watched her shaking fingers grab the cream-colored envelope.

By the time she was seated at a table for two, with a cup of black coffee, Shelley's hands grew still enough to remove the folded piece of paper.

> *My dear Michelle—I'm so sorry. A call came late last night from Matt and Kristy. Donna has taken a turn for the worse…*

Jeff wrote he was flying out early that morning, gave his address and phone number, asked her to get in touch upon return to the States.

Shelley swirled the coffee, gazing into its dark depths, feebly smiling when she thought of Ruth and the letdown to the story she would tell. Then, she decided not to tell Ruth. Relieved that no one she knew had shown up, Shelley tucked the letter in her purse—another souvenir—and prepared to leave. She would go to the Pantheon by herself. She would visit Victor Hugo and pay homage. She owned the whole day. She would try to spend it wisely, walking alone through the most romantic city in the world.

## *DUPLICATE*

*On another trip to France we visited a site called Guedelon Castle. It is a new construction project located in Treigny which is in the Burgundy region. It is being constructed with techniques and materials like those from the Middle Ages. Hopes are to complete it in the 2020s. When done it should be an authentic recreation of a thirteenth-century medieval castle. At the time of our visit around 2010 enough of the project was complete to give a very good feel for what was envisioned. I found the whole process to be fascinating. Soon after our return to our home in Seattle I started thinking about characters who might have spent a day at this intriguing locale. The place itself is the real part of this story. The characters and their circumstances are entirely from my imagination.*

# Duplicate

Published by *Marco Polo*, September 2011

Mother goaded me into coming to France. "A break from the stress of the past couple of years will be good for us," she said. By September 2009, it looked like the economy might be recovering. While we'd never recover from Dad's death, soldier-like, we carried on.

Mother still speaks of him so often it's as if he hangs over her shoulder, whispering instructions.

"I'll buy tickets tomorrow," she pushed. "We can go to Normandy after Paris."

Tempted, I said, "Let me know exact dates so I can organize time off."

"You're the boss, Tad. What's there to organize?"

Dad's people still fondly refer to him as "Dear old Al." Since I took over as president of MacPherson Building Supplies (in my mind an interim position) they can't do enough for me.

I've read a lot about Normandy, but to actually be there brought on unexpected feelings. Walking the cold beaches and entering intact bunkers, the frozen-in-time nature of Sainte-Mère-Eglise, with the paratrooper facsimile hanging from its church spire, the American cemetery that has a new visitor center honoring those who died. Mother made so many comments about Dad's days in Vietnam that I ended up saying, "He had nothing to do with D-Day."

Not one to back off, she said, "He felt proud to be in the military, no matter when."

After our too-short stay on the coast, she came up with a tour of this partially completed castle on our return to Paris. La Forteresse will become an exact replica of a structure inhabited eight hundred years ago. As we hauled suitcases out to the corridor by our adjoining rooms, she said, "I know with your love of history this will be a real treat, and the workmanship looks fascinating."

Unlike my father, building practices of all types hold little interest for me. Before our flight home to Seattle tomorrow, I had counted on a last meal at a Left Bank bistro, with a good bottle of wine. Something special before facing my future. Now, we'll have to settle for anything we can grab along the way.

At La Forteresse, stone walls rise above us maybe seventy-five feet. The castle keep is the first section to be built. This guy with dirty blond hair tied in a ponytail, dressed in tan jerkin and dark brown leggings, says, "I'm Jack, your tour guide." Obviously American. Like me, he looks somewhere around thirty. "Careful of the steps. No safety railings in olden times," he warns. We follow him to the top.

I take Mother's arm, but she brushes my hand away as though it's a bothersome fly.

Once we enter onto a flat roof, Jack gathers our group of ten or so at the winch and treadmill. Off to one side, masons, in clothes like his, all of them speaking French, pound and chisel and form stone blocks with ancient-looking tools.

"Your father would have loved this," Mother says.

"You think so?" Sure, my father, Alfred MacPherson, Sr., would have loved it if he had ever taken time for a vacation. I found him one night working late on a project, gasping for a last breath. He struggled to get out the words, "Take care of your mother."

"Absolutely!" she says. "He knew what it takes to build something substantial over decades. Doesn't this inspire you?"

"Sort of." Not at all. Plans are to complete the castle in twenty-five long years.

"To make his legacy even better?"

"Right." I decide not to go there, not here anyhow. Besides, with no alternatives what can I say?

Dad started his company in 1974, the year he married Mother. "It was my good fortune to find Sandra to help me," he used to tell people. She became his assistant, standing solidly behind him, putting in fourteen-hour days, even through her pregnancy with me. I spent my early years in a playpen next to her desk, yelping like a puppy until I learned that my cries generally were ignored. Their dedication to the business paid off. MacPherson's became an icon in the Seattle construction community, expanding to three locations. Before the crash, Home Depot opened another store in our vicinity, but longtime accounts have stuck with us.

"Castles were built of stone to withstand attack," Jack says. "As you can see by the pictures," brochures rustle, "ladders on the outside reached upper rooms. These were pulled in when enemies approached."

After Dad's heart attack, at Mother's insistence, I took a break from my contracted position teaching World War Two history at the university. She had long ago left the company in my father's capable hands, yet he continued to give her credit, saying things like, "Without my wife, I'd never have made such a success." Every summer all through school, I worked at the company. In Dad's absence, Mother assumed I'd take over. Rightfully so, I guess. I'm good at building (made all the bookshelves in my Madison Park condo). A person can be good at something he doesn't want to commit to for life, just like he can admire a person but not want to be him.

Jack shows us pie-shaped windows from which archers could shoot, and says that with the slanted walls, most returning arrows deflected, falling uselessly to the ground. Looking out, I notice a quarry and a draft horse hauling a wagon full of stones, clump of hoof after clump of hoof, straining against its harnesses with no other task in mind.

"There are fifty costumed people working here. If you have any questions, please ask someone."

From the time I could walk, Mother dressed me in overalls like a little carpenter. I had a canvas apron with plastic hammer, screwdriver, and wrench to go with my Fisher-Price workbench. As a kid, it felt right as a plumb line. When I got older, remarks about how much my long legs and deep voice reminded everyone of Dad, and how I'd keep the company going for future generations, began to grate. Eventually, I wanted to lash out with, "I don't look anything like him," when Mother would say, "Your features are becoming more defined—exactly like your father's."

"What's with the wagon down there?" an older man with florid skin asks.

"We're behind schedule." Jack grimaces. "The wagon got stuck in mud. Those stones have to be lifted up to this level with pulleys and winches."

We are told something about scaffolding made from wooden poles tied together to provide access. And then something about carpenters who use oak from the forest surrounding this castle. Timber supports are made out of wood that has been soaked in water all winter—to toughen it, which makes sawing difficult. Nearby, craftsmen carve decorative details on plaques. It's dusty work and several onlookers sneeze. After a few minutes given over to appreciating their efforts, Jack leads us to another wider stairway that goes down to the main area.

On the landing, he gestures to a closet-like opening, where a crude-looking seat is mounted over a shaft dropping down to below the ground. "By the 1200s, they added lavatories."

This room is next to the great hall. What about piles of shit and stench? What if a stray child slipped into the hole? It must have happened. Mother's not bothered. She's rubbing a hand over an archway, as carefully scrutinizing it as an architect searching for flaws.

We move into the cavernous room, where Jack says, "There'll be huge tapestries of the time. These took years to make, and were practical as well as beautiful. They kept out drafts." He points. "Through that archway will be a duplicate of long-ago royal apartments, away from the clamor."

And, the smells.

Before building the big house, we lived in cramped quarters on the floor above the company. I don't remember much about it, since we spent most of our time downstairs. After Dad really made it, he moved us to Broadmoor. There are so many rooms in that place, where Mother still lives, that I used to hide out for hours playing with my miniature military and naval figures, making pretend battles.

Jack waves his arms around and tells us about feasts and nobles at a long, elevated table. Others sat "below the salt," and around the lord according to rank. Servants ate afterward, mostly cooked vegetables. Their betters indulged in a spicy, rich diet consisting mainly of meat. "Jugglers, jesters, and minstrels provided entertainment. The fortune-teller hovered in a dark corner."

What would one predict for me? Despite Mother's arguments, I can't stay on at the company, and my university department head has moved me to the bottom of his instructor list. Little chance of getting another position, even if I wanted one.

"Tasters tested food to make sure it wasn't poisoned. Meat was served on thick slices of coarse brown bread fit inside silver plates. The bread soaked up grease and sauces, and was tossed out to beggars at the castle gates. Dogs sniffed around tables, searching out tidbits on the rush mats. For dessert, the nobles ate marzipan."

"Hmm, marzipan." Mother smiles. "I wonder what one of our dinners would be like in this kind of venue?" She'll probably have a medieval theme at her next party.

Several times a day, she's been calling for updates and to give suggestions, but she seldom comes into the office. Mother's now considered to be "company hostess," a duty she used to refer to as tedious—necessary, but not much fun. Recently, she said, "What would I do without your father, if not for these events."

Jack walks over to a wall. "This portion of the castle will be finished by the end of 2009 with forty roof trusses and twenty thousand tiles. Early financial records, illuminated manuscripts, cathedral stained-glass windows guide our work."

"Did any of those tasters die?" a boy with several cowlicks asks.

"Sure. That's why they got paid a lot. These heavily fortified castles provided protection against numerous enemies, but spies still infiltrated."

"Cool," the boy says.

"Let's move on to a storeroom."

The group fumbles into action, shifting backpacks and purses. We shuffle, single file, down another set of wall-hugging stone steps. I clasp my hand to Mother's thin waist, steadying her.

"I'm fine." She gives me a little shove. "I have wonderful balance."

I back off.

On the level below, Jack loops his thumbs into armholes of his jerkin like he owns the place. "Here, bags of grain, barrels of cider, fuel, and weapons were stored. When a castle was under siege, which might last for a year or more, inhabitants desperately needed all these things."

He looks at Mother, I'm sure noticing how she carries herself, like she owns the place, too. "When the lord went off to war, he could be gone for years. His lady ran the castle and community around it. She had to know about expenses, supplies, and giving commands."

Light shines in from a small, arched window. Jack says, "There'll be torches placed along all stairways. It'll be bright in here compared to the last room I'm going to show you."

Despite vaulted ceilings, I feel claustrophobic. The stone walls seem to be pushing closer to our group. Packed landing crafts heading toward Omaha Beach come to mind. Those men must have felt terrified. Another batch of tourists mingles at the top of the steps, waiting for us to sink further into the castle's depths.

"Before the cannon's invention in the fourteenth century, buildings like this were indestructible. Invaders attempted takeovers by hurling heavy stones against weak points, or digging tunnels to collapse walls. From siege towers they fired arrows into the courtyard. Defenders fought back with their own constant bombardment of arrows and boiling water poured on the besiegers' heads."

Jack looks around the room as if picturing stacks of provisions. "The people in the castle faced diseases like typhoid. They couldn't gauge the progress of battles. Running out of necessities meant either death from starvation or surrender to the enemy."

Members of our group scan the walls, their expressions uneasy. Maybe others are feeling hemmed in.

Not Mother. She's standing upright and sturdy as one of the support beams. Nodding, she says, "A commonsense arrangement."

"Captured enemies encountered dire fates. Beneath everything else in the castle were prisons, often built with only a hatch to the outside. Human beings could be cast into these holes with no possible escape. The French have a word for it. Oubliette—dungeon of oblivion."

I want to burst free. Mother lifts her head even higher. Apparently she's comfortable with the necessity for dungeons, probably thinking of executives from Home Depot.

"The prison I will show you isn't like that. It's a room where visitors can enter. Be extra careful of your footing. These steps are the narrowest."

I don't try to help her this time.

On the dungeon's wall are mounted rings where a prisoner's hands can be attached. Will there be instruments of torture? Catching my breath, I move to the edge of the crowd. How much longer will Jack ramble on?

"I'm sure some of you are uneasy. Think how an actual captive must have felt. Walk around that wall and you'll find an opening to the outside."

"Are you going to leave it like that?" the boy asks.

"Certainly. Tours of the castle are meant to be fun and informative. We don't want anyone passing out from anxiety."

Everyone else laughs. I'm going to be the first one out of this entrapment.

In the bright sunshine and fresh air, Jack says, "Time for me to leave. Come again to see La Forteresse grow."

I hand him a tip, and turn to Mother. "How about coffee?"

"Maybe I can find some more gifts."

For several minutes, I sit with my mug at a wooden table under a gnarly oak tree, watching costumed workers walk by. Tearing apart a croissant, flaky and buttery as those in Paris, I hear conversations of other tourists. A flock of birds flies overhead toward an opening in the forest that surrounds this site.

Mother brings her cup of coffee and places a large bag on the table. "I found a perfect tapestry reproduction." She spreads it out for me to see. There's a warrior with a hand on his lady's arm, ready to venture off. "It's time to go home. I don't have any more room in my suitcases."

Now or never. "If you have to leave some things, I'll send them to you."

"Send them?" Her face rumples in confusion. "What do you mean?"

"I'm staying."

"Here? At this castle?"

"No, but in France."

"For how long? What about the company?" Always the company.

"However long it takes."

"What takes?"

"For me to figure out what I want to do."

"I repeat…what about the company?"

"You can take care of it."

"Me?"

"You can take over as well as I can. Better. You helped build…"

"That was years ago. Do you want to let your father down?"

The sun warms my head, but her tone is icy. Still, I go on. "I know you can handle it. Like those ladies left behind when the lords went off to fight their wars. They managed—more than managed."

"You're deserting me, Tad."

I know she won't cry. Mother never cries. "They probably felt deserted, but they held down the fort for years at a time. You can, too."

She sips her coffee, deep in thought, possibly recalling those fourteen-hour days. Holding her chin higher, she says, "Can't I say anything to change your mind?"

"No. I'm certain."

"What about Home Depot?" She looks at me out of the corner of her brown eyes. Could there be a spark of excitement?

"You won't let them take away any of MacPherson's business. There'll be big sales. You'll cash in on the Broadmoor house, everything, before you give up."

With that, her brow etches in resolve. "What will you do?"

"I'm going back to Normandy. I have the background. I could become a tour guide."

"Little did I know that a trip to this medieval castle would change everything."

"Your life as much as mine."

## *WHYS*

*A re-written version of this story eventually became part of my novel,* Making It Work.

*Two main inspirations for the original story were the doll and my grandmother's unresolved grief. Like the older woman in the story, my grandmother won a doll, a beautiful doll. At the time, I was a young girl who had never owned a doll like that beautiful one. When I was an adult my grandmother gave the doll away—to a stranger. I was extremely hurt when my mother told me and I always wondered why Grandma did this. A jumping-off spot for a story. Also, my paternal grandfather died the year before I was born. He was shot under mysterious circumstances. Was it an accident? Murder? Or suicide? No one knew the answer. For insurance purposes it was deemed an accident. For the purposes of my story the grandfather's death was a suicide and the grandmother was full of whys to the end of her days.*

*"Whys" was published under the name Kay Harris.*

# *Whys*

Published by *riverSedge*, Fall 2011

A few years before her grandmother died, Sheila, now married but without any children, felt stunned, like a sparrow crashing into a window, when her mother said that Grandma had given The Doll away to some neighbor's granddaughter who came for a visit. These two were served coffee, milk, and cookies; then this girl played with The Doll, and ended up leaving with her.

"How could Grandma?" Sheila stared outside from her mother's kitchen, ignoring the crowded feeders and up-close, petunia-filled beds, concentrating on the tangle of undergrowth covering a hillside.

Grandma had told Mother that there were two granddaughters, and she didn't know who should get The Doll. So, she decided to give it to this little girl.

"To this unknown someone, who never even cared about The Doll, someone who knew nothing about her history—my history—with her?" Sheila tried to bellow, but instead, squeezing her eyes tightly shut, she whispered, "It's absurd."

Mother gave a pained shrug, unable to further explain her mother-in-law's peculiar decision. Grandma always said she loved Mother like a daughter, and they understood each other like best friends, but it didn't hold true this time.

Grandma also used to tell how the real grandfather sometimes got angry, his dark eyes becoming black, and left the house. He went for walks of several hours, all by himself. "When he came back, everything seemed better," Grandma said, with a lost expression. Sheila knew a long walk wouldn't help how she felt.

***

At only seven years old, she could tell this Minneapolis apartment had to be exactly like the last, except in this building's gloomy-as-a-cave basement. Daddy said it was going to be better, but Daddy always said that, just like he always told Mama each job would be better. Sheila knew differently. It had two bedrooms, the biggest for Mama and Daddy, with a window that overlooked a sidewalk so you could watch legs of people walking by; the smaller, in back of the kitchen, for Sheila and Tommy, her four-year-old brother. It smelled like day-old fried bacon.

"Where will I put my stuff so he doesn't ruin anything?"

"I'm going to hang a curtain, right down the middle of the room," Mama said.

"One side for Tommy, the other side for you. That'll keep him out of your belongings."

Sheila watched her mother draw a line in the air with her finger, then study the rest of the room.

On Sheila's side a window, way up by the ceiling, showed a row of garbage can bottoms; and on another wall, a door opened to the kitchen. Tommy didn't have a window or a door. "He'll come on my half to go in and out."

"We'll have rules. No touching Sheila's property."

Sheila looked skeptically at her mother. She didn't believe that Tommy, who tore up her books and pulled out the arms on her dolls, would ever follow any rules.

"You and I can paint a mural for him. It'll make him like it here." Mama smiled enthusiastically. "Won't that be fun?"

"What kind of mural?" The one at school had letters and numbers. Tommy would hate it.

"With animals. What kind do you think?"

"Monkeys." The jabbering, running-around, scuffling, wrecking-things monkeys behind bars at the zoo. Sheila wished for a cage to keep Tommy trapped in.

She had only two huggable toys left. One was a white, turning greenish, teddy bear. The green came from Vicks put on him when she lay in bed with a cold, being rubbed down regularly. When Mama said she had to keep braids and couldn't get a ducktail, Sheila chopped out a chunk of her own bangs, then victimized poor Teddy by cutting some of his hair down to the fabric. Worn holes around his neck let clumps of cotton spill out. Sometimes Mama, trying to salvage Teddy, stitched his head back in place.

Sheila's other toy, a rubber baby doll, drank water from a tiny bottle before wetting its diaper. With a ballpoint pen, she colored black circles in Baby's blank eyes. Dingy gray splotches from pressed-in dirt mottled Baby's pink skin. Crevices along its arms had worn through to crumbliness.

About this time, Sheila's grandmother won a doll from the Rebekah Lodge's raffle. Sixteen inches tall, with wavy, dark brown hair, blinking blue eyes, and moveable arms and legs, she didn't wet her pants. Accompanying The Doll came a varnished, wooden, two-section latched wardrobe case with a handle on top. Inside, drawers held shoes and boots and purses. A hanging area held outfits. Women of the Rebekah Lodge, sister organization to the Odd Fellows, where Grandpa Burt belonged, outdid themselves creating ensembles, while some handy Odd Fellow crafted the case. There was a wedding gown with little white satin slippers and a billowing veil; an Annie Oakley cowgirl costume—brown and gold with holster, pistols, hat, and boots; as well as a turquoise and white crocheted set with figure skates and beret complete with pom-pom—at least twenty-five costumes in all.

Grandma acted as excited as a little girl at winning this doll. She had grown up in a Catholic orphanage, with an absence of toys. "It held down jealousy," Grandma said.

Naturally, Sheila wondered why Grandma didn't give The Doll to her, being the favorite of many grandchildren, all the rest boys. But Mama said that Grandma wanted to keep her on the farm so Sheila would have something to play with on visits. Even at that young age, Sheila knew Grandma's life had been much harder than her own, and The Doll represented something very important—the only time Grandma ever won a prize.

Some of the upset women from the Rebekahs complained, "Why should an old lady, without any children at home, get The Doll?"

Grandma, perched on her chair at the dining room table, told the family this, shaking her head. "I said to them, 'I have a granddaughter. She can play with my doll.'" Then she huffed off to the kitchen after more mashed potatoes and gravy.

For years, the best treat was to go down to Grandma and Grandpa Burt's farm, away from inner-city pavement and a different apartment every year. On the many acres, Sheila ran free, and during quiet times played with The Doll, whispering all her secrets and plans. A picture in the bedroom where she slept showed a Victorian girl on a chair embroidering. She reminded Sheila of girls who took ballet and piano lessons at all her different schools. With The Doll, she pretended to stick pins from the Victorian girl's cushion in soft spots on her body.

Sheila was the firstborn grandchild, the one born to heal her grandmother's broken heart when the real grandfather unexpectedly died. That next spring, along came Sheila, Grandma's make-up gift from God. She never doubted how much Grandma loved her, because of her words, spoken every time they were together.

After the real grandfather died, Daddy and Mama lived with Grandma for a couple of years, at her old yellow house in Chambers, Minnesota. Sheila learned to walk in this house. Nearby was Grandpa Burt's farm, where she later played with The Doll. And Grandpa Burt's farm was by the real grandfather's farm. He had lost it, and every time they passed by on the way into town, Grandma said, "There's where we used to live, before your grandfather became a butcher."

Mama told about how Grandma was the only one who could comfort Sheila, a colicky infant.

Her grandmother snuggled the baby against large breasts, and within minutes, Sheila fell fast asleep. She came to think of them as Grandma's pillows. A miniature woman, no more than 4'8", with a little beak nose and arthritic knees that made her look like a barnyard hen, rocking back and forth as she walked, Grandma blamed the size of her bosom on the binding cloths forced upon her by the nuns when she developed too soon and too conspicuously. "All my muscles broke down," she said. "Mean things like that made me run away from that awful place."

Once when Sheila was about ten, living in another apartment with another shared bedroom in shambles, a Camp Fire Girl group Mother had signed her up for planned a program where each member would bring a favorite doll or stuffed animal to put on exhibit. All the toys she'd received at birthdays and Christmases, demolished by Tommy, had found their way to the trash on the next move—all except Teddy and Baby. She looked at them, feeling her cheeks redden with humiliation.

Mother said, "Don't worry. I'll write your grandmother and ask if you can have The Doll, for this one occasion."

They drove to the farm and brought The Doll back to the city. She and her paraphernalia made the best display, and Sheila won a blue ribbon. Tommy carried a threat from their father (Grandma's difficult child, the one who broke her pretties and caused her much grief) of a beating like never before if he did one thing to hurt Grandma's doll.

"Do you promise?" Dad said.

"I promise. I promise. I really, really promise," Tommy chanted.

He tried extra hard, and, for once, Sheila owned something special, even though it was temporary, that Tommy left alone.

All too soon, they brought The Doll back home.

Another granddaughter joined her family this same year, altering Sheila's status as the only girl grandchild. Being the oldest, and Grandma's favored replacement, however, made it easy to rationalize an ongoing importance. Besides, her little cousin ran with the boys all the time outside. Having plenty of her own well-cared-for toys, she never played with The Doll.

Eventually, makeup, and hairdos, and boyfriends entered Sheila's life. Dad had finally found a job he liked as an electrician, and moved them to a house to live in forever. And she had a private bedroom, where Tommy and his problems couldn't intrude. Sadness over broken, discarded possessions got pushed to the back of her mind. On visits to the farm, she sat in the corner, leafing through teenage magazines, trying to generate as little attention as possible. Too grown-up for swinging from ropes in the barn, or chasing sheep in the pasture, she also quit playing with The Doll, leaving it put away with Grandma's other treasures.

At dinner, Grandma still recited stories of how the real grandfather had unexpectedly died and left her bereft beyond belief. She continued to question (with reassurances from her children) if this was punishment because she'd left The Church. Still, God gave the baby girl to ease her pain.

Sheila fought back tears, trying not to embarrass herself in front of the whole family, a cloud enveloping her body, her throat feeling like it was stuffed with a bunched-up hanky. Dad had said, so many times, that "Sheila's bladder is too close to her eyeballs," making the boys laugh and tease. Much later, she figured out that he said this because of his own tingling, unshed tears.

Even during adolescent self-absorption, Sheila wondered about Grandpa Burt's good-natured acceptance of Grandma's need to take out all her woes, display them to the others, and then tuck them away for next time. She didn't see Grandma cry, either, but listened to her many words, always said in the same way. A kind and gentle man, Grandpa Burt shrugged at his wife's jibes about his favorite pastime—chuckling over a Reader's Digest, sitting in the wooden rocker with its scratched arms, where the real grandfather had solemnly dug lines with a matchstick.

As Sheila grew into adulthood, occasionally she thought of The Doll, smiled, and imagined a time when she would share her with a daughter, something that was never said to Grandma, just assumed…

So, she never understood. Too hurt, too afraid of crying, Sheila never asked why Grandma hadn't thought how she would feel when The Doll was given away.

Eventually, Sheila had her own little boy to care for, and was too preoccupied to give The Doll much consideration. When he was six months old, she brought him 1,500 miles from Seattle to visit Grandma and Grandpa Burt, who had retired and now lived in Chambers, in the old yellow house. An easy baby, mostly smiling and charming the world, he took a bottle, willingly, eagerly, from Grandma. Afterward, he snuggled up to her pillows and drifted off, while Sheila marveled at the never-ending technique. She also noticed that since Grandpa Burt's heart attack, Grandma had quit talking about the real grandfather.

By the time of a baby girl's birth, Grandma had died, and Sheila again started missing The Doll. Consequently, her own daughter had as many toys as any little girl could ever want, in a beautiful pink-and-white room—the room she came home to as an infant and left from when she went to college. Even now, even though the daughter has lived in many different cities, shelves in that old room are laden with dolls in various elaborate costumes. She liked them, but mostly cherished her Barbies, spending endless hours changing their clothes and combing their hair. By modern standards, maybe The Doll wouldn't have been that remarkable. From Sheila's little-girl perspective, she was loved so much that, of course, she became real.

***

Sheila hopes the neighbor's granddaughter cared for The Doll at least half as much as she did. And she hopes that, maybe even now, that grown woman tells stories about the little old lady friend of her grandmother's, the one with the pillowlike bosom, who not only gave her cookies and a super-soft hug, but also, a wonderful toy.

Sheila believes that Grandma let go of her need to know, a need far greater than Sheila's own question. It started the day she found him, dead of a gunshot wound. No note. No reason. No answer for her "whys?" And, many years later, after speaking of him hundreds of times, she decided enough words had been said.

Sheila feels the familiar cloud and closed-up throat set in, but this time they go away, with wet cheeks and a sob, as she grieves for the lost doll and her grandmother's sorrows. Looking out through blurred eyes at her own garden, bordered by cascading petunias, with the sun shining brightly, she knows this: Today is a good day for weeding.

♦

## *TURNAROUND*

*Several years ago I went on a trip to Ireland with my son and daughter. Since I was the only one over twenty-five I got to be the driver. My twenty-one-year-old son would have done a much better job. The three of us, as well as the rental car—a red Opel—survived intact with me driving on the opposite side of the road. The Slea Head Drive was particularly memorable and months later, at home, I started this story using that as an inspiration. Because the whole driving experience, through one thousand miles of The Republic, was tension-filled, the character's own set of tensions came relatively easily.*

# *Turnaround*

Published by *The Writer's Workshop Review*, March 2012

We're having a hearty Sunday breakfast of oatmeal, eggs, and bangers served by Mr. Harrigan, the widowed innkeeper, when Devin, his son on holiday from Cork, drops by our table. He wears a cobalt blue shirt that sets off near-black eyes and thick, dark hair. "You're from that grand town of Boston."

My sister Leslie doesn't answer, continuing to push food about with a fork. I say, "Our father's relatives sailed there from Galway."

"Do you like Dingle?"

"When we first got here it seemed the most traditional of spots." If only Leslie would take over, but she doesn't. "Until we saw Oceanworld and Fungi."

"Ah, that tourist attraction with its bottle-nosed dolphin. You'll have to take in a few pubs with a bit of folk music and set dancing."

I glance at Leslie's downturned face framed in thick blonde curls, and reach up to adjust a barrette that keeps my own ash brown strands in place, "I've been wanting to hear more Irish tunes…for my students."

"Musicians you are. Then, it's a must."

Leslie doesn't bother to tell him she's in real estate.

"Maybe. After our drive."

When he's out of earshot, she mumbles, "I don't feel like that sort of thing."

Will she ever feel like anything? Two years ago, before Daniel was killed, Devin Harrigan would have gotten a full dose of her attention. For Danny, a quiet guy, being married to Leslie meant watching her, mascaraed eyes flashing, captivating others. He never seemed to mind because they were a team.

I can't help but remember my senior prom, over ten years ago. Her address book overflowed. After several tries with boys who had asked but failed to take her to dances, she finally found a presentable date for me. He had a toothy smile and Leslie called him a "great friend."

I scrape up the last bite of my meal. Leslie's barely touched hers.

A short while later, Mr. Harrigan ambles over to our car, where I'm fidgeting in the driver's seat.

"Follow the sign after the bridge." He gives a wobbly-fingered point to a board, hand-lettered in black, which says Slea Head Drive, Ceann Sleibhe. He pulls off a tweed cap and scratches his head, then leans down to peer in the car. Is he concerned about my ability to comprehend directions? Or, is he worried about Leslie, who sits unblinking, adrift in the passenger seat?

"Don't know if you'll get out much, with the damp, but you'll be dead impressed by the drive. Watch for the soft margin. And, the sheep!"

I start our burgundy-colored Opel with its unfamiliar stick shift. The man at a Hertz counter in Dublin promised it would be a "breeze" to drive. Somehow, even with driving on the opposite side of the road, I've managed to get us around Ireland to this fishing village on the west coast.

Devin walks out of the inn's yellow door, staring at Leslie the way men always do, their faces lighting up as if turned on by a switch. She never glances his way.

I put the car in gear and roll smoothly toward the street, pebbles crunching on the driveway. Maybe I'm getting used to this.

Mr. Harrigan touches his forehead in a salute and Devin waves.

"The innkeeper's son likes you," I say.

Leslie's glazed blue eyes focus on the opaque sky. "Why would you say that, Noreen?"

"A look about him."

"Maybe it's for you."

I don't bother responding to this silly notion.

Through the curtain of mist, hedges of pink and red fuchsias mingle with a multitude of green hues. Fuzzy outlines give an aura of timelessness. How can this magic escape her? Our left front tire veers into the soft margin. I straighten the wheel, and squint through gathering fog. Ahead, a trio of goats stands nonchalantly on an 18-inch stone wall above Ventry Bay. One fellow has only three legs. Just beyond, there's a flicker of our first view. I brake the car, steering clear of the soft margin. "How 'bout we take a look?"

"I can see enough."

"Years ago, 'Ryan's Daughter' was filmed here."

She doesn't budge.

Standing by myself, I recall that on this very beach the wayward girl, in her long black skirt, strolled with ruffled parasol held high. The sand looked like gold dust. Sprays of moisture tickle my face and I pull my Gore-Tex jacket's hood tighter. What would it be like to walk on this beach in the sunshine? To run barefoot in the warm, sparkling sand?

"Are we going to keep moving?" Leslie's peeved voice intrudes on my musings.

I get back in the car and keep driving. Not much to say about the fog. Then, on a grassy hillside to the right, I see something. "Look! A sheep!" I hand the annotated map to her. "What's it say about them?"

"There are 500,000 sheep on Dingle Peninsula which is part of County Kerry," she singsongs. "That one seems kind of lonesome. I wonder where all the others are?" Since Danny's fatal car accident, Leslie hasn't reached out to, or shown interest in, anyone or anything. She's taken leave from the office.

"Bring our Leslie home," Mom whispered, when we said good-bye at Logan. She knows what it's like to be a widow since Dad passed away over ten years ago. Leslie used to be exactly like him. They were the larks to Mom's and my sparrows.

We're coming on a sign that reads Taisteaal go Mall.

"What's the map say this means?"

"Drive Slowly. There's a school." She gestures to a deserted yellow building. Ghostly kids seem to be running on the playground. Leslie gazes at two swings swaying in the wind as if only recently left behind. First came the accident, followed by the miscarriage.

I try to pull her attention back to more earthly matters with, "You must be hungry. Mr. Harrigan told me about eating places at the turnaround."

No response.

Moving on, we pass relics built into the slopes. Leslie begrudgingly reads about a Stone Age Ring Fort, dating from 500 BC, referred to as a 'fairy enclave.' The locals' effort to retain their first language of Gaelic, as well as these ancient structures, touches me. It makes up for Fungi.

Odd-looking beehive huts called 'clochans,' resembling stone igloos, dot the landscape. There are over four hundred in the area. Early ones sheltered monks who fled to Ireland's wilderness, saving Christianity from extinction. I feel a twinge of admiration for their sense of purpose.

"Let's walk up to one of these."

"They look awfully dank." Leslie wrinkles her nose.

We reach a clochan and upon entering, I rub my hand along its rough, dry wall. "Should smell mildewed, but the way they're built, 'corbelled,' keeps them dry." I sense the presence of a long-ago huddled holy figure. "Can you picture living in here?"

"Too well." She backs into the rain, me following a few minutes later.

Around some more curves, I spot the site for which this drive is named. "We're at Slea Head," I announce, feeling like a tourbus guide. There's a large white figure of Christ with the three grieving women at His feet. "We're on the westernmost point of Europe. People say the next parish is Boston."

I'm closer to home than anywhere else on our journey. Waves crash over rocks below. The ocean, visible for only a short distance, disappears into a dense curtain of rolling gray.

"A ship called the Santa Maria de la Rosa sank out there." I'm reminded of Devin Harrigan's dark good looks, defining the term Black Irishman. "It was part of the Spanish Ar...."

"That statue is horrible!"

"Why?"

"There's red paint streaked on the hands and feet. Even the body. To look like blood." I stare at the blotches and agree they're disturbing. Still, I feel something else. "Maybe someone was trying to get closer to the pain. Make the story more real."

"Why would anyone want to do that?"

"Life has been wretched for these people. This gives them hope."

"It makes me sick. When Danny died and the baby...I went to church..."

I think of our mother's Episcopal Church where you'd never see statues like these.

"It was useless," she goes on. "Why did God do this to us? I don't know what Mom was thinking. Why would this place, with its gloomy weather, bizarre traditions and morbid religion make me feel better?"

"We were grasping. Maybe something about Grandpa's Ireland might console you."

"Can't you understand? I don't want to be consoled."

"We better go. There's still over half the loop to make."

When she discovered her pregnancy, Leslie assumed I would babysit on weekends, saying, "You could use something to do."

"I'm plenty busy," I said, but other than preparing for my music classes, I sat alone with the TV most evenings.

Through swishing windshield wipers, there's an occasional glimpse of reclaimed land-patches where rock walls support grass growing from transported sand and seaweed. We come upon stone structures sprouting from the earth. Some are inhabited. Others fall in shambles, abandoned eons ago. It's the loosely-connected village of Dunquin, Dun Chaoin.

Ahead, I spot a middle-aged woman riding a bicycle up the hill. "Wonder how far she has to pedal?"

"Looks abysmal."

The woman wears a plastic rain hat. Several layers of handmade cardigans partially cover her dark print housedress.

"Don't females here believe in wearing pants?" Leslie frowns at the woman's mud-splattered bare legs. Anklets skim the tops of her brogues. Features bunched, eyes straight ahead, her shoulders bob back and forth. Behind her, a herding dog trots, ignoring the rain.

As our car passes, I raise a hand and smile, but the woman doesn't respond. It's the first time on this trip that Ireland's legendary friendliness proves absent. She perseveres as if in a trance. The dog wags his tail and barks when we cruise by.

"Not curious, I guess."

"Good for her. The cheeriness in this country gets to me." Leslie scowls at the woman she just praised. "Her mind's on the task at hand." The old Leslie would have wheedled an acknowledgment.

Back on the drive, I spot a herd of black and white cows, plugging along toward us. They ooze around our car, engulfing it. Against side windows gigantic heads rub slimy smudges. Eyes roll sideways, looking with no real interest, while an acrid odor seeps inside.

"Must be lunch time. Nothing's going to keep them from the barn."

"They're determined. Galumphing. A step at a time." Leslie's head bobs. Then, "Here comes that woman."

This time, she walks her bicycle around the herd, brushing by a roadside building, passing so close that I hear water sloshing in her shoes. As before, her eyes stay straight ahead. Not even a wink for our shared predicament. The dog weaves in and out between manure-encrusted legs, mindful of a kicking hoof.

Shortly after leaving the cows behind, the woman and her dog wend their way down a driveway toward a cottage. A mile or so later, we arrive at the turnaround where another sign indicates two different roads will bring us back to Dingle Town, 11 km either direction. The dreariness of the day has succumbed to darkness. I'm tired and wet and hungry. Without consulting Leslie, I head right, away from the ocean, and search for somewhere to eat.

Down this road, with hazy fields on both sides, I spot a shake-covered building, smoke drifting from its chimney. The parking area is empty. Inside, the comforting aroma of meat and vegetables simmering fills the room. A woman with a mantle of gray frizzy hair and pale pointed features greets us with, "Failte." Welcome. She leads the way to a table tucked next to a fire. "I'll bring tea?"

"Thank you." Beside me is a bookshelf. I pick up an autobiography by Peig Sayers documenting hardships of life in the nearby Blasket Islands, Na Blascaodai.

"Did you enjoy our drive?" Leslie asks.

Taken aback by her interest, I say, "Yes, a lot. I'd like to come back again when it's clear."

She doesn't ask when.

"Did you like it?" I refrain from saying *at all.*

"Eventually." She blows on her tea.

"When did that change?"

"It was the woman on her bicycle. And those silly cows." A small, long-absent smile fleetingly appears. "Their persistence despite the weather."

"No matter how difficult the day."

"She didn't feel the need to be friendly or pleasant. Blast the rest of the world."

"She was..."

"There's always been this expectation that I would be charming. Delighting everyone. Taking charge." Leslie looks through a window at the falling rain. "I can't do that anymore."

Her eyes meet mine, holding steady. I see watery blue with gray and green. They used to dart excitedly, from person to person, never resting long enough for this kind of scrutiny.

"You're always going to be miserable?"

"I'm not miserable."

"What are you then?"

"I'm sad and angry."

The woman with the cloud of gray hair returns, carrying a basket of bread and lamb stew in earth-toned pottery she says is made locally.

When she leaves, Leslie sits forward. "I always got what I wanted. I didn't think about it much." She goes within for a moment. "Now, I don't want anything except..." She takes a deep breath. "I want you to stop watching me, hanging on my every word, as if at any moment the real Leslie will suddenly materialize. She's gone."

I feel as though she's taken my shoulders and given me a shake.

"I'm lost and I don't have a hint where I'm going. I can't very well show you."

As we continue silently eating, the door opens, and in walks Devin Harrigan, his dark hair sparkling with raindrops. He smiles broadly and strides our way.

"I saw the Opel. Glad you're well. Da fretted when the weather changed."

"How thoughtful of you to come checking on us."

"'Tis nothing. I needed to set his mind at ease."

"We didn't have any problems, except for a herd of cows." I laugh.

"It's hard to come this way and not get stalled by one type of animal or another, but I was sure all would be well. You were in complete control when you left."

Devin declines my offer of stew. "I'll join you in a cup of tea." He pulls up a chair and rests his arm on our table.

Other than a greeting, Leslie doesn't say a word, for which I'm unexpectedly grateful. Tones from a piper begin to float through the background. It's "Londonderry Air," a piece I played at the memorial service. Listening, I'm surprised not to feel like crying for Danny or clinging to Leslie.

I tell Devin about the three-legged goat. "That'd be the Scanlons'," he says. "There're many roaming these hills, but only one like him." And, with a grin, "That fellow's almost as much of a curiosity as Fungi back in town. Maybe they should charge for viewings." Then, "Speaking of town, how about a round of pubs and Irish music?"

"I'd rather settle in with my book," Leslie says immediately.

"Noreen?" Devin's look of anticipation never wavers.

"I'll decide when we get back to the inn."

There's still the rest of the loop to drive and plenty of soft margin along the way, but I'm already looking forward to joining him. For the music, of course. Singing the lilting ballads and dancing a carefree jig, on Devin Harrigan's strong, bent arm.

## TWO AGAINST ONE

*My husband and I have aided our four parents in their elderly years with much love and much concern. The most difficult one had alcohol-induced dementia, which came and went. This parent lived to be ninety. One of the innumerable challenges involved a willing move into a retirement home and then, five week later, while we were on vacation, a contact made with Starving Student Movers. This small business transported all possessions back to the original house. It was the spark that ignited the story. Each character and his or her circumstances is entirely made up, but the concern for an elderly parent is not. It's a problem for many of us who have loved ones in jeopardy.*

# Two Against One

Published by *Epiphany*, June 2012

Hilda Reinhardt flopped onto a plastic and metal chair, knocking into the office's pale green wall with a bang. Her feet planted firmly on the floor, her arms crossed over a massive chest, her broad shoulders pushed the chair's back erratically. Hilda's daughter, Hope, hunched because of scoliosis, sat next to her in an identical chair, ankles crossed, hands folded. She gazed at a picture with abstract shapes in soothing pastel colors while they waited for the doctor to finish reading Hilda's chart and give a diagnosis.

Hope was an only child. Her deceased father, Oscar, had been an electrical engineer. Hilda was a retired civil engineer. She had left a German immigrant family and begun training for her profession in the days when women didn't do such work. Oscar, also a German immigrant, and Hilda planned for their "Hope" to become, at the very least, a fine architect. They later always referred to her chosen field as "one of those 'ologies."

At Chambers Community College, Hope taught sociology, a position she loved, rationalizing that she'd never married, at soon-to-be forty, even though she'd been proposed to many times, because of devotion to her students. A longtime boyfriend, Jasper Strand, also an only child, who she saw once a week on Saturday after his chores were done around the house, was an anthropology instructor at the same school, and lived in an apartment over his widowed mother's garage.

They spent time together at Hope's townhouse, away from Mrs. Strand's watchfulness.

After several minutes, Dr. Marlys DeGuise looked up from the test results, probably trying to figure out how best to broach the subjects indicated. "Your MRI and brain imaging show abnormalities compared to the tests administered five years ago."

"What kind of abnormalities?" Hilda barked.

"Now, Hildagarde, I know this is hard for you to hear. You've always been so organized, so on top of things, so in control, but I have to tell you there's been changes."

"What kind of changes?"

Hope reached over and put her hand gently on Hilda's knee.

Hilda jerked away.

Hope sighed. Personality traits often strengthen, like wine or vinegar, as a person ages.

"Vascular disease with extremely high blood pressure. You are not getting enough flow to your brain."

"I feel exactly like I've always felt."

"That's part of it. You know, this is called the Silent Killer." Dr. DeGuise paused and looked at Hope, who only gave a slight shrug. "It's imperative that alterations to your life be made sooner rather than later."

"What kind of alterations?"

"You need to stop driv…"

"Stop driving? I just bought a new car!" Hilda's Honda Accord was five years old. She had purchased it after going in the ditch and totaling her Buick—thankfully, with no injuries. A fireman and a police officer called to the scene failed to detect alcohol on her breath.

This was a familiar smell to Hope, who despite Hilda's protestations of "Don't contact my daughter!" had immediately been located and came to the accident site. Medical tests soon after showed everything to be normal, and she reasoned that her mother, after a noon drink, must have fallen asleep at the wheel. This was the first time, ever, for Hope to issue a directive to her mother: No drinking and driving!

"With blood pressure in the two hundred range, you could have a major stroke at any time," Dr. DeGuise went on. "Lose control of your car. Kill an innocent bystander."

"Hmmmpf." Hilda's pressed lips failed to soften.

"And, you need to move into a retirement ho…"

"Retirement home!"

"Someplace where your meds and readings can be supervised daily."

"You mean assisted living." Then, "I do a fine job taking care of my pills. Each morning I swallow them with toast and coffee."

Hope didn't mention chauffeuring her mother to Minneapolis for the MRI and brain imaging. They had started off in the early morning. Hilda forgot to eat breakfast and take medicines because of the shift in her routine. By 6:00 p.m. when Hope got her back home, Hilda's systolic pressure had shot up to two hundred and eleven.

For fifteen minutes, she and Dr. DeGuise verbally sparred. The doctor took every stance trying to convince her 85-year-old patient of what needed to be done, always focusing on blood pressure as opposed to memory loss. Hilda relentlessly insisted she was fine and fully able to take care of herself in the house where she had lived for almost fifty years. "I'm going to leave feet first and not breathing. Until that time, I will not give up my automobile."

Looking at her watch, Dr. DeGuise said, "I have another patient waiting, Hildagarde. You must make these changes as soon as possible." Then, turning to Hope, "Do you have anything to add?"

"Only that Mother's drinking seems to exaggerate her forgetfulness."

"I barely drink a drop!"

"How much is a drop?"

"One at my noon meal. Oscar and I always did this."

"What kind?"

"A glass of wine…sometimes a martini."

"How much alcohol?" When Hilda didn't answer, Dr. DeGuise held her thumb and pointer finger up, first with a space of one inch between them. "This much?" She stretched the space into at least three inches. "This much?"

Hilda clenched her hands into fists and refused to answer again.

"I'm not going to say you cannot have a drink. A glass of wine with your main meal—four ounces—is fine. But it will be in the retirement home dining room."

"I'm not going to that place."

"It's absolutely necessary." Dr. DeGuise clapped the file shut.

"What about her forgetfulness?" Hope recalled countless missed engagements.

"Approximately thirty percent of all people who reach Hildagarde's age experience moderate memory impairment. This may turn into Alzheimer's, but I'm not concerned about that right now. The blood pressure needs to be controlled or your mother won't be around. She'll either be in a nursing home, completely disabled, or in a funeral par…"

With a grunt, Hilda lumbered to a standing position, grabbed her big black purse, and marched out of the room, purposefully neglecting to say good-bye. The automatic door clattered shut.

"You're going to have a hard time," Dr. DeGuise said.

"Tell me about it!" Hope clasped her hands tightly, as if in prayer. "I don't know how this possibly will be accomplished."

"Do you have any siblings?"

"No, I'm all alone."

"Call me if you need assistance. In the meantime, get her signed up to move into Pheasant's Nest as soon as possible."

Chambers, Minnesota had one retirement/assisted living facility. Hope put her mother on their list for an apartment immediately after the car accident. But every time availabilities came up, Hilda told Burt Anderson, the manager, that she wasn't ever going to leave her house.

Hope told him, "Please keep calling. Mother possibly will have to relent. I just hope a crisis that causes this won't be too bad."

While she worried about a fall or a stroke or another car accident, the years slipped by. At last, it was the diagnosis of vascular disease with accompanying dementia that forced a decision. This also pushed Hope into a place she had never been before—arbiter of her mother's well-being.

The next day, she met with Burt and signed paperwork to rent an apartment the beginning of July. Hope had a month to prepare.

First came several visits with Hilda to see all that Pheasant's Nest offered: three nutritious meals along with snacks; a van that took residents on outings for supplies, doctor's appointments, and interesting places like Red River Valley Casino or an afternoon symphony at the Chambers Performance Hall; and, most importantly, a nurse on duty at all times to monitor her health.

Hilda stomped through the halls, bellowing things like "Pheasant's Nest. Whoever came up with that stupid name?" And, "All these cripples wobbling around on walkers." And, "This place smells like dirty old people."

Hope whispered things like "We have lots of pheasants around here. I think it's a nice name." And, "Mother, please, you'll hurt their feelings." And, "It's the disinfectant. They have laundry service provided for residents and apartment cleaning once a week."

Hilda resisted with things like "I will not live someplace that sounds like it belongs in the aviary of a zoo." And, "They're probably deaf too." And, "You act like I can't manage my own chores."

During Hope's daily phone conversation to make sure her mother was still among the living, after much useless coaxing, she realized the car would have to be taken away without consent. Late one Saturday afternoon, she made a surprise visit to her mother's house with Jasper (his assigned duties completed) tagging along for help and support.

"What are you two doing here?" Hilda, still in her old gray housecoat, seemed surprised to see Hope and sneered at Jasper. That Casper Milktoast boyfriend. No wonder my daughter won't marry him, she'd often said.

"We're taking the car." Hope held shaking hands behind her S-curved spine.

Hilda stumbled for a rack in the kitchen where she and Oscar had always hung their keys. Grabbing the set for the Honda, balance regained, she charged toward her bedroom with Hope in hot pursuit.

"I don't want to have to take them. Please give them to me, Mother."

"You can't have my car. I won't let you. I called the sheriff and he said you can't take it away from me."

With the power of attorney her mother had signed shortly after Oscar's death of brain cancer, when Hilda was still thinking rationally, Hope was almost, but not quite, certain no one would keep her from carrying out this task. While Hilda still looked as substantial as ever, arthritis had stolen the strength from her fingers. One big yank and Hope took possession of the keys, tossed them to Jasper, and the two of them made a beeline for the garage. Jasper backed the Honda out and followed Hope in her Subaru to an auto parts store, where she purchased a device called The Club #3000 to disable the steering wheel in case Hilda plodded over to the townhouse and tried to drive off in her car.

There were times when she picked up the phone and immediately hung up on Hope. There were other days when she called many times, leaving troubling messages if Hope was out: reasserting that she would not move to Pheasant's Nest, stating that the sheriff would back her up, and boasting that she still had her legs to go anywhere she wanted to go.

Hope tried to reason with her mother but, after repeatedly covering the same territory, came to the conclusion that Hilda would only hear what she wanted to hear.

On another Saturday, in the morning, leaving Jasper's mother miffed about unwashed windows, the pair arrived at the house. Hope directed which furniture to put on the truck while Hilda clumped behind, repeating her mantra, "I will not leave my house!"

The movers had serviced other clients going to Pheasant's Nest and seemed blasé about Hilda's recalcitrance, even when she grabbed one by the arm, causing him to drop an end table.

Jasper hovered next to her, distracting with comments about "downsizing." And, "living more simply." And, "how much easier life will be." Hilda shot back with "You are annoying as all hell." And, "Stop driving me crazy with your nonsense." And, "Shut up, you twerp."

Jasper, bless his heart, continued the nonstop banter, and after three hours, a loaded truck headed for the retirement home. In her Subaru, Hope, Jasper, and Hilda (fuming in the backseat about having "to retrieve my belongings") brought up the rear.

Once there, Burt kept her in the lobby with talk about an addition that soon would be started and structural problems encountered. Like a tag team, Hope hurried through instructions for each piece of furniture's placement as Jasper stood guard in the apartment's entrance.

At the all-clear sign, Burt brought Hilda to her new home. "Doesn't this look great? Your daughter did a wonderful job arranging things."

"Tell those movers to come back here this minute." Hilda glared at her Trinitron television, her bookshelf to be loaded with manuals, and her cabinet that would hold awards received from various engineering projects.

"We're leaving." Hope grabbed Jasper's arm and they bolted for the exit as Burt said, "Hilda, let's take a look at the construction site. Maybe you'll have some suggestions."

That night, Hope and Jasper toasted each other with a favorite merlot. Somehow, according to a phone call from Burt, Hilda had been settled in for her first night's sleep at Pheasant's Nest. About this time, a conclusion was reached. Jasper's 86-year-old mother, a cantankerous retired schoolteacher, had begun to constantly make the same remarks and lose her keys and forget to bathe. She would be joining Hilda at Pheasant's Nest before too much longer. Hope and Jasper's first joint effort seemed to have succeeded. Feeling positive about a similar win with Mrs. Strand, they shared another toast.

The next morning, the couple left in the Subaru for a trip to Bemidji, a town in Minnesota's far north. After a spontaneous hurry-up wedding they embarked upon a weeklong camping trip in order to decompress. However, before starting the drive into no-cell-phone country, Hope parked near the statues of Paul Bunyan with his mighty blue ox and called Pheasant's Nest. The report was not good. Hildagarde had gone missing in action, presumably to squat at her old, mostly empty, house.

Jasper said, "I know this has been brutal, but we must turn around, return her to Pheasant's Nest, secure the residence." He held Hope against his concave chest as she wept, completely dampening his buttoned-to-the neck, pale blue polo shirt.

At a pause in her tears, between hiccups, she snuffled, "There'll be more butting of heads. Her dementia's not keeping Mother from going another round."

### SKULLS

*My husband and I took a trip to Germany, Switzerland, and Austria several years ago. Hallstatt, Austria is an exquisite town that I will always remember and one of the things that intrigued me was the Charnel House at the local Catholic Church. My husband had no interest, nor did anyone else on our tour, so I hiked up there by myself. Usually I find cemeteries and mortuaries to be disturbing, but every once in a while I'm drawn to explore this sort of place. It was the case with the Charnel House. Something drew me to it, and thus the story "Skulls" was inspired. The rest of the story is fictional, but the details at the cemetery and Charnel House are as I remember them.*

# Skulls

Published by *Wild Violet*, October 2012

Their delicious late lunch of bratwurst, sauerkraut, rye bread, and light beer had come to an end. Megan pushed her chair back from the table with a scraping noise on the scratched wood floor. "It's now or never." The next morning they would be leaving.

"Do you mind going up there by yourself?" Alex asked. "My feet are killing me." His new walking shoes had proven to be too tight. "Besides, I've seen enough churches." Together, they'd visited at least ten cathedrals and chapels on this trip — on Alex's part, because of an appreciation for history and beautiful architecture, not because of any heartfelt belief.

"I'll be fine by myself." Surely there'd be other tourists.

Megan and Alex had been in Hallstatt for two days, staying at an old hotel with high-ceilinged suites overlooking one of Austria's deepest, most beautiful lakes. From their balcony, they could see mist-shrouded mountains encircling this lake, casting mysterious shadows along its banks. Upon their arrival, the couple had taken a boat ride showcasing the exquisite village. They'd held hands — hers rough and red from a bout of eczema; his strong and clasping. Occasionally, he'd let go to take pictures of clustered wood-frame chalets, snow-covered peaks rising above them, the bridge over a half-hidden lagoon. In between, he had picked her hand right back up.

They left the rathskeller, and Alex went to sit on a bench by a burbling fountain in the village's square. Megan left him, long legs stretched out, sunlight beaming down on his brown, wavy hair, eyes closed. This trip had been a welcome break for both of them. Several months before, Alex had taken over his father's Seattle surgical practice, with its benefits and responsibilities. Megan loved teaching first grade, but twenty-five children could often be demanding. They'd been married at his parents' country club (with a judge friend officiating) five years before, and hadn't vacationed since a short honeymoon in Vancouver, Canada. In addition to a rejuvenating change of scenery, they hoped that this time away might result in what they wanted most: to start their family.

***

Walking away from the square on the village's one road, Megan searched dense foliage covering the hillside for a way up to the church. After what amounted to a couple of blocks, she found a door-size opening in the leaves with the beginning of a moss-covered stairway. No signs indicated that this was the right place, but she decided to take a chance. Making the first zigzag, she wondered, Will I stumble into someone's yard? Climbing and swerving and climbing some more, her breathing became labored. There must have been at least a hundred steps. With each blind curve, she doubted whether this was the correct way. Should I turn back?

At last, her trek led to the parish cemetery's rock-bordered graves. These plots closed in near to the church, with barely a few inches of space unoccupied. Megan tiptoed through them, each planted with red geraniums that looked like splotches of blood. She'd read that over two centuries before, because of limited land atop this hill, and in order to make room for more bodies, each one was kept in its grave for only about ten years. Before burying a newcomer, an existing plot had to be dug up. The former resident's bones were bleached in the sun and stored in the adjacent Charnel House.

These graves didn't bother her too much. Since she was six years old, Megan had, on many occasions, visited the cemetery where her mother was buried, often alone. Still, relief enveloped her when she arrived at the doors to the small church that towered over the village. As expected, they were unlocked. She stepped inside, stopped for a few seconds, and took in traces of incense while her eyes adjusted to the darkness. She dipped her fingers into a marble font and crossed herself with holy water. Feeling like an intruder because she had broken so many rules, at the same time her heartbeat and breathing steadied, her shoulders softened, like resting in her mother's arms when distraught over a friend's rebuke, a criticism from a teacher, ripping a favorite blouse. She was often drawn to a Catholic church, like an anxious patient prescribed Valium the night before surgery.

As she always did, Megan lit a candle at the statue of Mary and the Christ child, praying first for her never-to-be born baby, then for her absent mother, and next for her father, a retired construction worker who seldom left his cluttered house, only going out for paltry groceries and a supply of liquor. Watching the wavering flame, a faint smell of smoke surrounding it, she included Matthew, her good Catholic first husband who, in the way of her father, had cared for his booze more than he cared for her.

She knelt and under her breath recited childhood prayers — Our Father, Hail Mary — and the comforting Twenty-third Psalm. Because she was far away from home, Megan whispered, "Please give us a safe return. Keep us from any disasters." A terrorist bombing; a hotel fire; a crashing airplane. So many things frightened her, but she wanted to go wherever Alex went.

Gazing at the altar and stained-glass windows and crucifix in this silent sanctuary, she recalled other opulent ones they had recently seen — the magnificent cathedral in Trier with its pilgrim's walk to the golden chapel where a relic supposed to be Christ's robe was kept; Munich with its baroque interior and statue forever fighting a Protestant demon; Mondsee with its heavy rococo embellishments where a virginal Maria from The Sound of Music walked down the aisle accompanied by the sisters' heavenly voices. Megan had been drawn to these places like a fish to a sparkling lure. Hallstatt's church seemed unimpressive in comparison, but after so much abundance, she preferred its simplicity.

Delaying the reason why she had come, Megan began to consider criticisms of the Church's wealth. She had never before seen Old World extravagance, and rationalized about all the good that had been done in Catholicism's name. Still, how much more could be done for the hungry and the sick and the needy if money spent on maintaining these immense temples was used for them?

Her last prayer before leaving was: "Please God, let me get pregnant." Megan had made this request every day since she married Alex.

He wanted a baby as much as she did, and knew about her past, often reassuring her with comments like, "I did plenty when I was young. All that time in juvie. Selling drugs to kids at Lakeside. Think of the people I hurt." And he would say, "If you could just relax...." Tests on both of them had given positive results. Nevertheless, she failed to conceive, and often thought, How exactly am I supposed to relax?

When she left the church, Megan poked a twenty euro bill in its offering box, and felt less like a trespasser.

An arched entrance to the Charnel House stood maybe five hundred feet away. Ready to stop the procrastination, she headed in that direction, eyes locked on its ornately-carved double doors. Then, as if a force pushed her back, she whirled and returned to the church's safety. Leaning against its stone wall, hands limp at her sides, she peeked at an official-looking old lady who wandered the grounds — the only other person Megan had seen. She wanted to approach her, but what could she say? "Will you please go in there with me?" What if the lady slammed the doors and locked her inside? Megan smiled at this ridiculous notion, but her uneasiness persisted, like being caught in a canoe going against a rushing current. She pulled out a tattered guidebook from her backpack. A yellow Post-it marked this site. Leafing through the entry, her eyes stayed unfocused as her head tilted toward a blurred page.

***

She pictured her father, whose presence generally lurked right below the surface of her mind. When he was in the midst of a drunken binge, Megan went to church and prayed, What am I going to do for him? And hoped for a solution. Before leaving on this trip, he'd failed to answer his telephone for several days. She'd let herself into his house unannounced, and found him passed out on the living room sofa with the television blaring. Smelling like he hadn't taken a shower in a week, when finally roused, his words had been jumbled. She and Alex had planned to go soon. Feeling imprisoned without any key, she'd gone to Mass. Afterward, she'd hired a home-care worker recommended in parish literature to check on him each day — care for him if emergency help was required; or, with his alarmingly high blood pressure (her heart felt like it would explode at this concern), care for matters, should he die.

Whenever he recovered from one of these terrible episodes, with his face drooping down to his collar, he would always say, "I'm so sorry. Please forgive me. I promise not to do it again." Then, he'd pour bottles of whiskey down his kitchen sink.

Having heard this so often, Megan had started to fight an impulse to say, "Shut up. I don't believe you. Prove it to me."

\*\*\*

She closed the unread guidebook and rubbed her itchy hands. If someone else came to visit the Charnel House, which would close shortly, she could go up to the guardian lady and buy a ticket, then tag along. This seemed strange — to pay — but what other draw did the small church have?

There was a gently sloped back path that she had discovered after climbing the formidable stairway. Now, trying to decide if she should forget about her mission and take the easier way down, Megan chided herself for absurdity. She would stay a little while longer. Afternoon's golden yellow made the tombstones glow. She put on sunglasses in order to secretly study the guardian lady, who appeared to be fifty or so, with a face scrunched into judgmental lines, like the matron at a women's detention center. She wore a gray jacket with a gray mid-calf length skirt, heavy hose, and serviceable shoes. Patrolling the area, she stooped to retrieve a piece of litter here, pluck a faded red bloom there. Did it bother her to be in the midst of so much death? Had she followed every rule? Did she have children?

\*\*\*

After dug-up bones were bleached in the sun, mourners painted symbolic decorations like laurel for valor and roses for love upon each skull, along with a name, date of birth, and date of death. Megan imagined pink roses for her mother and her unborn baby. The fetus had a beating heart in its tiny chest, and a developing brain inside its soft, forming skull, and a nourishing cord attached to her. Was there a soul? The Church said so.

Like the Nocturnal House at Seattle's Woodland Park Zoo with its scary snakes, some of them gigantic, reading about Hallstatt's macabre resting place fixated Megan. In the Nocturnal House, living creatures — a ten-foot boa constrictor, for one — wriggled and blinked at onlookers. It was hot and humid. Plexiglass walls protected viewers and occupants alike. A claustrophobic, dimly-lit aisle wended its way through the exhibits. She would brace herself to go in. The kids on her field trips jostled and giggled and sometimes blocked her way. Feeling like she might hyperventilate, Megan would push through them, moving toward an exit. Not noticing it was their teacher, the first graders yelled things like, "Hey, watch out!" At the end, she inspected discarded shells and skins in display cases, waiting for the children to finish their explorations. In her classroom, she taught reading, suggesting answers to endless questions, letting them come to personal conclusions. Each year, on each field trip, she chose once again to go in the Nocturnal House.

***

After her mother died from ovarian cancer, nuns and her parish priest looked out for Megan. These people of the Church gave treats of chocolate, praise for high grades, and encouragement when, after promising differently, her father never showed up for plays and programs attended by everyone else's parents. Their administrations helped, even though often she was so filled up with tears that Megan feared the dam would crack and humiliate her. Like most little Catholic girls, she contemplated becoming a nun until boys started paying her the attention she craved more. Megan had an abortion at seventeen. Soon, she was to leave for college. She went alone to the procedure, not sure of the baby's father, but certain that she couldn't continue to be chained to her own father.

***

After several more minutes, with a sigh of regret, she decided to leave the churchyard. Megan glanced toward the path, but chose the stairway. It would be easier going down. About ten steps into her descent, she heard someone clumping around a curve. Another chance! If this was a visitor to the Charnel House, she would go in, too. She saw his brown hair, and a moment later, his dear face. Alex had come to find her. "I'm so glad you're here." She held out her roughened hand to him.

"That was quite a hike," he said.

"On your poor, sore feet."

"I got worried. Don't want anybody to abduct my sweetie."

"There's another easier way."

"We got some more exercise." His mouth lifted in a crooked grin.

"I've seen everything... except for the Charnel House."

"That's why you climbed up here." Earlier, he'd asked, "What's the fascination with a bunch of old bones?" To which, shrugging, she had no answer.

"Will you go in there with me?"

"Sure. I'll save you from hobgoblins."

Alex paid the three euros to the guardian lady, who said in heavily accented English, "He's here, heh?" She didn't look the least bit scary up close, rather like a tired housekeeper. With his hand at her waist, Megan and Alex crossed over the Charnel House's threshold.

Because it was built into the hillside, she had worried that it would be a catacombs-type tunnel with flickering wall sconces. The actual room was small, probably not much larger than a mausoleum, and well lit. Instead of shelves with coffins, slanted racks — similar to those in a supermarket used to show off cabbages and other produce — displayed the skulls. She halfway expected sprigs of parsley to be tucked in beside them. There were no small ones — remainders of lost children. What happened to them? Hers had met the fate of all medical waste. She placed a red, flaky hand over her middle.

The lower jawbones were mostly missing. She assumed these came unhinged and were stored with larger bones stacked like kindling and firewood below the skulls. For several minutes, she checked out eye sockets and nose cavities, read names and inscriptions — noted these details as she might examine craft items at a county fair.

When Alex asked, "Are you ready to leave?" Megan felt no inclination. "You go ahead. I'll be out soon."

A crucifix hung above the racks. Once alone, she felt no urge to pray either. The odorless room was clean and seemingly free of dust. Maybe the guardian lady spent time with a collecting cloth, polishing pates when she wasn't tidying the yard. Did many other curious people visit here? Most of the bones were ancient. Perhaps only a few people in Hallstatt still cared.

One recent addition, a woman's skull, had a gold tooth lodged in the upper portion of what used to be her mouth. She was the last one to be included at the shrine. In the '60s, with the acceptance of cremation by the Catholic Church, bodies were transported to Salzburg for the process. Sometime in the '80s, apparently not looking forward to this prospect, the woman was granted a place in the Charnel House.

Did the guardian lady ever question what happened to the souls once encased in these skulls? Would she make a special request to be placed here as compensation for her devotion and labors? Did she live with a guilt so strong that, in guarding the Charnel House, she did her penance?

Megan touched the top of her own fine blond hair, moved the hand to her forehead (remembering years' worth of smudged ashes), rubbed fingers in sockets that held her blue eyes, slid them over cheekbones, bumped across a mole, and came to rest at her pointed chin. The hard bones beneath her warm skin felt cushioned. She placed the hand on a pulse at her neck.

Megan had been protected from witnessing dead bodies. Her father kept her from looking in the casket at her mother's remains. A vacuum-like device had rapidly sucked the fetus from her womb. Textbook illustrations showed them to have disproportionately huge heads and eyes.

She reached out and placed a finger on the woman's skull. It was cold and hard and smooth as ivory, like a carved box her mother had used to store meaningful writings. Sometimes Megan read them, trying to feel closer. She took the yellow Post-it from her pocket. This one was by Byron as he contemplated a skull: "Look on its broken arch, its ruin'd wall/Its chambers desolate, and portals foul/Yet this was once Ambition's airy hall/The dome of Thought, the palace of the Soul."

Her soul still resided within. She was still alive. Not perfect, but with all the possibilities for change and growth. At that moment, something closed inside Megan as something else opened.

***

When she left the Charnel House, the guardian lady sat hunched over her desktop, maybe concentrating on accounts, seemingly oblivious to why people visited there.

Alex waited for Megan, standing patiently near the church's stone wall.

Bells began to chime for five o'clock. "Should we take the easy way down?" she said.

"Steps are fine with me."

"Your poor feet."

"Plenty of time to rest them on our flight home."

Her breathing slowed, her shoulders softened as they descended the stairway hand in hand. Surprisingly, hers felt less inflamed. His was still strong and clasping.

◆

## *ROMAN-IRISH BATHS*

*On a trip to Germany we stayed in Baden-Baden. It would never have occurred to me to visit the Roman-Irish Baths which I knew were experienced in the nude, with men and women together. However, there was a woman on our tour who got about seven other women, including myself, interested in going as a group. I was amazed at how freeing this happened to be. I didn't feel at all uncomfortable that there were men and women together in the different pools. The Germans are so blasé about such things. In fact, our group of women did irritate some of the local ladies with our giggles which we quickly suppressed. One woman in our group told me before we went in that she felt uncomfortable because of a recent mastectomy. I assured her that we all had our imperfections and that she was brave to come with us. This was the inspiration for the story. The rest is pure fiction.*

# Roman-Irish Baths

Published by *Amarillo Bay*, February 2014

Molly's brown eyes squinted open. Dimmed lights barely illuminated wavering shapes, like peering through a sheer, billowing curtain. Wrapped in a heated blanket, arms scrunched against her sides, she wiggled her fingers.

A woman said, "That's good. You're coming to."

Focusing to the right, Molly noticed an empty chair. She clumped her heavy-as-a-bowling-ball head in that direction. Another bed— empty. Sloshing back to the center, she took a ragged breath and strained to lift herself. A throbbing, burning sensation radiated from the left side of her chest.

The woman wore a baggy pink top with comical bears leering at Molly.

*Where am I?*

A stethoscope hung around the bear woman's neck.

A disinfectant smell…Seattle General.

"We'll have you to a room in a snap." The woman flopped down on the chair and took Molly's wrist. "Pulse fine. You're in Recovery. How do you feel?"

"Left side…it's hot." As if to dispute this statement, Molly shivered and goose bumps rose on her arms.

"Normal. We'll get you on more pain meds."

"Normal for what?"

"Honey, I'm sorry. Doctor did a mastectomy."

Mas…oh my God.

Molly yanked away from the nurse and rubbed a hand across her chest. Right side full as ever. Left side…no left side. "He didn't think …"

"I know, honey. Once in there he decided this was for the best."

"The best?"

"He told you it might happen."

"He said 'a remote possibility.' Probably a . . . lumpectomy."

"I'm sorry, honey. That wasn't enough."

"What's with the honey stuff? Is this Winnie the Pooh country? Where's my husband?" Beginning to tremble, Molly felt not a twinge of guilt for her rudeness.

"He'll see you shortly." The nurse lumbered out.

A male orderly in blue scrubs, sans comical faces, tucked the blankets around Molly. "You'll settle down soon."

Will they knock me out again?

He rolled her bed down a hallway to a private room, hooked her up to some machines, and quietly left. A window framed flowering trees.

Jeff appeared at the doorway.

"They're certain it's all gone." He walked to Molly's bedside and put a hand on her shoulder, and with a voice slow and strong, "You'll be good as new…after treatment."

"No!" She pulled away. "Did they tell you he cut off…"

"You're going to be fine. I love you. We'll have many more years together."

Molly looked out the window. "Akebono Cherries," she whispered.

"What?"

"The trees. They're Akebono Cherries."

"Before long you can go home to your own Akebono Cherries."

"When?"

"A few days." He kissed the top of her head. "I want to stay longer, but that nurse, the one big as a grizzly, ordered more rest."

After he left, Molly threw off the blanket and placed a still-shaking hand over her left side, like pledging allegiance. Her heart felt closer than it had ever felt before, and the burning increased. She stared at the trees, their pale pink blossoms rustling with a breeze, and felt the beginning of deep, desperate sobs.

***

She'd been a tiny kid—in every class picture the one placed front and center. Both of her small parents often told Molly, "Be careful of those big kids down the block."

Once, at twelve, she forgot to lock the bathroom door before hopping into a shower, and her oblivious father barged in. She shrieked as if an ax murderer had entered.

"For God's sake, Molly," he hollered. "You're scrawny as a chicken."

Her friends started wearing bras by sixth grade. Molly pinned cotton balls to the inside of her lace-edged undershirts. When she forgot to take them out before tossing one in the laundry, she overheard her mother laughing with a friend. "Molly wants to have a bra so bad that she's stuffing her undershirts!"

After that, she skipped the cotton balls and practiced cartwheels instead.

Freshman year, she made the varsity cheerleading squad. Her parents fretted about injuries, while the older girls teased about having a "spunky attitude." They'd toss her to the top of pyramids with little effort. She'd stand there, all four foot eight and eighty pounds, arms stretched out like a high diver ready to soar, with a red-and-blue uniform top lying flat against her chest. She never lost her balance, but did fall hard for Luke Palmer, power forward on the basketball team. When he asked her to Winter Ball, she felt ecstatic as an Olympian. That is until Anne Turner, squad captain, said, "He's shy. He'll feel comfortable with you."

College proved to be the same. Other girls in her sorority complained about gaining so much weight their first year, from macaroni and chips and frat party drinking. Molly stayed at five feet and ninety-five pounds until graduation.

Concentrating on her horticulture degree, she'd tell sisters, "He's okay. Very polite," when downplaying that the only guys who asked her out were socially stunted and barely five feet tall themselves. Sticking to her studies, Molly's passion became trees.

After receiving her diploma, she apprenticed to a landscaping company; and, all of a sudden, it happened. At twenty-three years old, Molly gained her Freshman Fifteen and grew four inches. Still small by most standards, amazingly, at least five of those pounds popped out to give her C-cup breasts. Her dad whistled when she strutted by. Her mother said, "I always knew you took after Grandma."

Molly began to attract attention from guys who were interested in more than taking care of a little sister substitute.

Her friends would moan, "It's so hard to find dates out here in the real world," while Molly smiled to herself.

After a hectic year of work and too many late nights with too many different guys, she met Jeff. Tall, with hair the color of burnished autumn leaves and skin ruddy from hours outdoors, he loved trees as much as she did—big trees, little trees, deciduous trees, evergreen trees, flowering trees, fruit-bearing trees. And, he adored her.

Molly decided, This is the one!

They started a small nursery—he was the outside man; she was the counter person and bookkeeper. Jeff told her, "You know so much about our business and are great with the customers."

Eventually, they had two boys, both of them robust nursers. Several of her friends experienced problems breast-feeding. Not Molly. And, much to her pleasure, the boys resembled tall Jeff. When they took vacations in Maui, the heavy-lidded glances of men at her in a bikini didn't escape notice by either Molly or Jeff.

He relished that people found his wife to be attractive, especially as they crept toward middle age and lots of her friends turned frumpy. He'd say, "You're just as gorgeous as the day we met."

About the time of her forty-fifth birthday, however, she received a diagnosis of breast cancer.

After the surgery, Jeff continued to take her in his arms and tell her, "You really do it for me, Moll," but she wondered, Is this just reassurance?

In spite of his words, she again felt like that tiny girl who everyone hovered over.

And now, I'm deformed.

***

Because of an infection, the doctor said, "Reconstructive surgery has to be put off."

"It doesn't matter." Molly wanted her left breast to exactly match her right—nothing less.

Before they went out for a movie one evening, Jeff sized her up in a baggy tunic and said, "How come you never wear any of those pretty sweaters?"

With her special bra she could have, but said, "This is in style."

"Oh…right."

The hospital sponsored a mastectomy support group that, with Jeff's encouragement, she attended—once. A poor woman who looked about twenty-five squished a wadded tissue to her eyes and said, "My husband doesn't ever want to make love to me."

Molly pitied her, but would have preferred if Jeff stayed away. Where once she'd been playfully enthusiastic and uninhibited—doing a cheerleader striptease—she'd started to silently curve her body to his, snail-like, and place her upper arm in a certain crooked way, attempting to make the missing breast less apparent.

Apparently trying to help her relax, he'd say, "You're perfect—exactly like you are."

She wished he'd hurry up.

Several months after the surgery, he began talking about a trip to Germany for Oktoberfest. A bowling buddy and his wife wanted to go with them. Both guys were beer drinkers, and they called this "an excellent way to kick off the fall."

Jeff and Molly had joked around with Bob and Michele, a busty blonde, at Husky tailgate parties, but they weren't close. Ordinarily, Molly would have done research and worked out itineraries. Instead, she ignored their plans. Suspecting that Jeff had come up with this trip as some sort of therapy, she wished for an earthquake or a terrorist attack.

"We don't have to stay that long in Munich. We can travel all over the Black Forest. Go to Baden-Baden. Trier. Anywhere we want. It won't be all about beer." Jeff's enticing tone flopped.

Still, with no national disasters, before she knew it, Molly found herself on a Lufthansa flight from Seattle to Frankfurt with the other three laughing in anticipation while she forced a smile.

***

She did enjoy Munich's botanical garden, glockenspiel, and jolly street singers; but the jam-packed city, with exuberant people in pastel-and-white checkered shirts and dirndl dresses, proved to be overwhelming. Men looked like giant elves in lederhosen and leather boots. Women's bodices were so low that their enviable boobs oozed out like creamy soufflés. Michele bought a festive blouse and fit right in at the Hofbräuhaus. Molly stuck with tunics that hit at the collarbone, even when sweat dripped between her good breast and her bad breast in the crowded, steamy white tents on the festival grounds. Despite this, she tapped a foot to oom-pah-pah music, but refused to dance a polka when Jeff asked.

Bob didn't suggest this to Michele, and she confided to a surprised Molly, "I don't like to dance."

Something in common besides detesting beer.

The guys lifted their steins another time.

After three days of this, Molly lightened up as she gazed out from their train at the heavily treed landscape beside tracks heading toward Baden-Baden. That is until Michele, sitting next to her, mentioned the Roman-Irish Baths. "We can spend an afternoon at them. It's supposed to be the most relaxing thing you could ever want to do."

"What about the casino?" Molly hedged. She wondered how much Jeff had told them about her surgery. These baths were done completely in the nude, and no way would she participate.

"We can gamble tonight."

Back in their hotel room, Molly told Jeff, "I hated group showers after gym class in high school." She took hers wrapped in a beach towel. "I'm not going."

"Why not try it? When in Baden-Baden…"

"Some of the pools have men and women together." She cringed. Then, "Are you going?"

"Sure. It'll be interesting—different than anything at home."

"I think I'm going to be sick."

"We can walk around town tomorrow. Maybe by afternoon you'll want to brave it. I'll be with you."

Exhausted from carousing in Munich and visiting Baden-Baden's opulent casino, where everyone lost at the tables, they went to bed early. What little sleep Molly managed to get was full of smothering cleavage and cherry-red nipples.

***

Next morning, they trekked up and down hills, the three others jabbering about sights while Molly remained silent. Michele stumbled on the cobbled streets, and Molly, in high-heeled sandals, also had to catch her balance several times. After a few hours of this, she barely touched a lunch of bratwurst and sauerkraut.

Before heading off to the baths, Jeff said, "I'd sure like you to come along."

Michele agreed. "It'd be great to have you with me—for moral support."

"Absolutely not." Molly sped back to the hotel room, where she flipped through a novel, tried to decipher a German television program, and tossed back and forth on the bed, with her eyes wide open, hoping for a nap. Finally, she removed all her clothes and did something she hadn't done since the surgery—studied herself in the mirror. She'd lost weight. Her arms were firm and thin. Her legs were tan and strong. The small mound where her breast had been was smooth and pink and harmless-looking. She took in her whole image and ignored what was missing. Not that bad. She quickly dressed and took off toward the baths.

After paying forty-three euros for the full treatment, she put a blue bracelet with a locker security device on her wrist and went to the changing rooms. Once stripped down, she wrapped a large white sheet around herself. A group of stark-naked women were walking out the door.

All that skin! She tried not to ogle.

In the first area, a husky girl wearing white shirt and shorts took Molly's sheet and said in English, "Have a shower."

Under one of many spigots, Molly huddled, among at least nine other bare women. Ducking her head and hunching her shoulders and bending her knees, she tried to be as inobtrusive as possible, feeling like that scrawny chicken kid. A few moments later, she realized that no one was looking at her. This was like parochial school with its uniform equalizers. There was a woman with pendulous breasts hanging almost to her belly button; a woman with a sagging stomach scarred by a caesarean; a woman with legs heavily patterned by lumpy blue varicose veins. A couple of young, seemingly flawless, beauties were the exception.

Molly went through a sauna and a steam room much faster than the instruction board recommended, trying to catch up with Michele. Another shower came next. This time she stood with normal posture, before moving on to a ten-minute salt rubdown that couldn't be hurried. It started out flat on her back. This was the closest anyone but the doctor had seen Molly's altered body. Midway, the masseuse told her to flip over, and she heard the woman make hushed, commiserating sounds over her knotted shoulders. With a quick slap to Molly's butt, she signaled the rubdown's end, and Molly felt a wistful pang.

After a few more stops, she reached the first pool with men as well as women, and there floated Michele, arms resting on the sides, eyes closed, large breasts buoyant in the water. Molly glanced across the pool, where a few men lounged. Jeff grinned and waved. Bob, from tact or embarrassment, kept his eyes on the vaulted ceiling's whimsical murals. She nodded, slipped into the pool, and greeted Michele with a tap on the arm.

"I'm so glad you came," she said.

"This is quite a place."

"Pretty freeing, don't you think?" Then, when Molly didn't answer, "This has been a hard year, hasn't it?"

She does know. And, Michele could see for herself. "Horrible." Molly started to tear up.

Michele placed a hand on her tensed shoulder and gently pushed it down. "Take a deep breath. There's nothing to be ashamed of."

That motion, those words, did more to ease Molly's tightness than anything else had done, even the massage. Breathing slowly and deeply, her shoulders released their grip on her neck. Her arms relaxed against the side of the pool. Her legs rose out in front of Molly, as if iron weights had been unlocked from the ankles. Floating thus, she imagined an angelfish, its fins and tail feathering across the water.

"I'm going to the other pool." Michele paddled to the steps.

Molly watched as her new friend got out. Watched her long, straight back. Watched her firm, smooth thighs . . . and . . . something looked amiss. What was wrong with her right leg? Why did she have a latex cover on it? Michele had an artificial limb that started above her knee. Molly had only seen her in pants, and the occasional slight limp she'd attributed to sore feet from sightseeing.

Suddenly, losing all self-consciousness, Molly got out, stretched tall, with her shoulders back, and walked over to join Michele in the smaller pool. Feigning German nonchalance, the two women paid little attention to their husbands, except for arched glances, when they splashed in. Molly and Michele stayed quiet, absorbing the healing waters. After half an hour or so, as if of one mind, they emerged and exited to the right.

Their final shower, followed by plenty of lotion, preceded the best part yet. In a dimly lit room, with single beds lining its walls, they were cocooned in warmed blankets and left to rest. Molly touched the left side of her chest. A gentle bump. She touched the right side. Soft and full. She ran her hands down her lonely body. Slowly, she slipped into a refreshing, light sleep, filled with dreams of pressing up to Jeff.

# JOB SEARCH

*This story came before my novel,* Making It Work. *It was inspired by a job search I had when I first moved to Long Beach, California. This was a miserable time. In reality, if I didn't get a job I would have to leave my husband who was in the Navy and go back home. We had only been married a few months. Even though the events, as well as the characters, in my novel are from my imagination, I observed many different types of people and situations during that time. This story is a fictionalized account of my efforts to find employment. While the actions and office settings are imaginary, the emotions are true.*

## *Job Search*

Published by *Rio Grande Review*, Spring 2014

From the time Sheila started working, when she was a high school sophomore, every job she ever applied for had been hers, because her father, Carl Doty, did electrical work for numerous businesses in Minneapolis. When she first wanted an after-school job, he said, "I'll find you something. I've got lots of connections." He turned on his one hundred-watt smile. Soon she was hired as a part-time elevator operator at Pfeiffer's Department Store. It mirrored her up and mostly down moods regarding her father.

The beginning of July 1965, Sheila, aged nineteen, arrived in Long Beach with Jim Gallagher, her sailor husband. The first Monday, after finding a place to live, she stood at the State Employment Office's glass entrance door, studying her reflection. Dimpled prettiness back home might not pass muster in glamorous California. Running fingers through her freshly washed, curly red hair, she worried, Has it started to frizz? She'd spent a lot of time pressing her homemade aqua polyester dress, but wondered, Does the hem look uneven? It was 9 a.m. and she wanted to be the first applicant of the week. Sheila pushed open the door.

An hour later, after a grammar and typing test, she met Mr. Bosanka, the man on whom her hopes were pinned. Middle-aged, he had a shiny pate with a graying fringe, deep furrows between tired brown eyes, and several extra pounds stuffed into a worn, tan gabardine suit. As she sat in the chair next to his desk, leafing through a government pamphlet, Sheila sensed when he looked up from her scores.

"Unfortunately, Douglas Aircraft isn't hiring," he said.

Not knowing anything about this company, she didn't ask. She tucked the pamphlet in her black patent leather purse and waited for him to go on.

"They should resume in a month or so. Meanwhile I'll send you out on some other interviews. Your qualifications are good. Ordinarily it wouldn't take long to find you a spot. Right now I don't have a lot of openings…with summer vacations and all."

"I really need a job. If I don't find something soon, I'll have to go back to Minneapolis. Jim and I haven't been married that long. He's in the Navy. Enlisted. On a ship." She took a deep breath.

A low-ranking sailor like Jim only made enough money to support his own needs, and Sheila's allotment check of $100 a month was going to barely cover her rent.

She watched Mr. Bosanka's eyes move to the photograph on his desk of a woman and a trio of girls. One of them, cute with a flipped hairdo, looked like her high school friends.

His tone softened. "Don't worry. I'll find a job for you." He picked a few cards from his file box, made a couple of calls, and several minutes later handed her a yellow appointment slip.

"Thank you so much. I really appreciate it. I can't wait to go to work."

\*\*\*

Jim returned home early that evening, carrying a cardboard pizza box. "Ship's going out on maneuvers tomorrow. Be gone three days."

Dreading another absence, Sheila threw her arms around him, squishing the box against his chest.

"Whoa, girl!" He backed off. "Watch out for the Whites."

He changed to jeans and a faded T-shirt with "Minnesota Twins" stretched across his chest, and they started eating pizza, sitting cross-legged on the efficiency apartment's Murphy bed that they always kept down from the wall.

"How'd the appointment go?" Even with tomato sauce dripping on his square chin, Jim looked as handsome as ever.

Instead of planting a kiss on his messy face, Sheila told him, "Mr. Bosanka's a nice man, kind of fatherly, in a good way, but there aren't a lot of jobs at the moment." Her stomach clenched and she put her slice of pizza back in the box.

"It won't take long. Remember how fast you got on at the bank?"

Being reminded of First Federal brought on a wince. "If California doesn't pan out," her old boss, a school buddy of her father's, had said, "your job will be waiting."

"I have an appointment. Maybe I'll find something right away."

***

Two anxious weeks and three unsuccessful job interviews later—one wanted accounting background, another decided to hire from within, and the last chose to eliminate their position—Mr. Bosanka sent her to an uptown law firm that was looking for a girl to assist their office manager.

Upon entering through the heavy double doors, Sheila, even though she was barely 5'2" and weighed less than a hundred pounds, felt clumsy and out of place. In special moments Jim called her his "little doll." This always made her feel cherished and protected. Nothing could make her feel good in this situation.

A meticulously kept desk made of polished, light-colored wood dominated the airy reception room. Behind it sat a woman, straight-backed, with platinum-blonde hair cut in a short, waved style. Tastefully applied makeup accentuated her raised eyebrows. Completing a scan of Sheila, she sniffed. "You must be," turning to the note in front of her, "Sheila Gallagher…from State."

Sheila gave a quick nod. Why didn't I take more time with the hem on this dress?

"Or are you delivering something?"

"No. I'm Sheila Gallagher. I'm applying for your job."

"Louise Hewett." The woman slipped a long, graceful hand with bright-red fingernails across Sheila's palm, fast, as if she didn't want to contaminate herself. "I'm Mr. Briggs' and Mr. Newell's office manager." She pointed to a wooden accent wall behind her desk with two names in shiny brass letters mounted under a royal-looking insignia. "I certainly hope this works out. We've been trying for months to hire someone. Here's an application and you need to type a letter. Follow me."

She stood and stroked her purple silk scarf before leading Sheila past a pair of offices with glass windows in their doors. Sheila peeked in one. A fellow with crinkly, near-black hair never raised his head from the paperwork in front of him.

Near the end of the hall, wide windows overlooked a courtyard garden full of unfamiliar tropical plants. Louise Hewett turned left into a small room without any windows, even in the door. It had a gray metal desk and a swivel chair, an IBM Selectric typewriter with a piece of white paper rolled into it, and a strange-looking black box. File cabinets closed in around the desk and chair.

"You can sit here. This will be my assistant's office." Louise Hewett handed Sheila the application. "Fill this out."

Sheila took it, hoping the office manager didn't notice her own chewed fingernails.

Louise Hewett opened a drawer and took out a headset. "There's a letter on the Dictaphone, ready to go." Apparently noticing Sheila's dismay, she paused. "You do know how to operate a Dictaphone?"

"Oh, sure, yes, I do."

"I'll return in thirty minutes." She swooshed around, brushing against Sheila's bare arm with the smooth gray fabric of her swirling skirt, leaving a cloud of expensive-smelling perfume in her wake.

While listing pertinent information on the form, Sheila began to shiver. The air conditioner operated at full blast, and with the door shut this room felt like a walk-in freezer. Thankful that the application was brief, she placed it aside and, with shaking hands, turned to the Dictaphone.

She discovered how to hook the head apparatus up, then squished the band over her unruly hair and turned the switch on. Dead silence. How do I hear the recording? Despite the icy temperature she began to perspire, tiny drops forming on her upper lip, as if she were in the midst of a humid Minneapolis day. What time is it? Fifteen minutes left?

Rubbing damp palms on her lap, she produced two lines of gray down the front of her dress. Oh great! Fiddling around with the nasty little machine had made her fingers dirty.

With a deep breath, she tried to collect her thoughts. A cord, hooked on the box's back, ran down a wall behind the desk. Sheila yanked at it until a pedal dislodged.

This pedal, similar to the one on her sewing machine back home, was divided in half. Tentatively she pressed the right side with the toe of her black patent leather sandal. Louise Hewett's withering voice said, "Letter to Mrs. Raymond Robertson, 555 Ocean Terrace, Long Beach. Dear Mrs. Robert…"

Sheila had started typing right away and there was "Letter to" at the top of the page. *Why didn't I listen for a minute? What was she going to do for another piece of paper?* Her heart pounded and her throat constricted. *I can't go ask that woman for more.*

She searched every drawer of the desk and finally found a small stack. Sheila rolled one into the typewriter. *Oh God, it's crooked.* She loosened the ratchet and made an adjustment. There were thumbprints on the page. The platen made a clicking sound as she yanked the smudged paper out. She'd forgotten to put tissues in her purse. Taking another sheet of paper, she proceeded to press it against her fingers, then stuffed it in back of the typewriter. *I'll get it later.* Sheila jiggled one more sheet straight, rolled it into the typewriter, and restarted the Dictaphone.

"…son: This is to inform you that we have sent notification to your neighbor regarding his fence…"

She lifted her foot. The letter resumed where she had released pressure. *How to backtrack? It had to be the other half of the pedal.* She tapped left, then tapped right.

"…his fence…"

*Not far enough.*

She pushed left, a little longer.

"…cation to your…" *Still not far enough.* Sheila pressed her foot down a long while. *I have to reach the beginning.*

"…look forward to seeing…" *What happened to Mrs. Robertson's problem fence? It was another letter.* She touched the right side of the pedal, gingerly.

"With warm…" tap, tap.

"…cerely," tap, tap.

"...ney at Law." This must be the end. Holding the forward half of the pedal down, she waited through a few quiet moments before she heard Louise Hewett breathing, followed by, "Letter to..." The start!

Sheila typed Mrs. Raymond Robertson, dropped down a line for the address, then she saw—no date. Should she put one above the name? Centered? That seemed right. She started to type July 19, 1965, and ended up with "Julu." She searched the middle drawer. No White-out. No Correct Type. One gray, rough eraser. Working on the "u," she pressed too hard. A hole! Why did I type the date?

Sheila tore this paper out. Clickety—clickety—clickety. She put another piece in and started over again, with a sour taste in her mouth, like she might throw up.

She got down to "Long Beach" before making another error. Dad was right! I'll never get a job.

Next time, the mistake happened before she got through Mrs. Raymond Robertson. I'm going to have to go back to Minneapolis.

She put the last sheet of paper in and started typing the date. As she pushed the return to begin that same address, the door opened, letting in her fragrance—lemony.

Louise Hewett said, "Time's up. Give me your work."

Sheila looked at the crisscrossed, messed-up papers, carefully removed the last sheet from the typewriter, and handed it, with the others, to the office manager.

"Well, I never!" Louise Hewett said. "And your application?"

"It's somewhere in there." Sheila suddenly felt her failed deodorant. Cold, wet rings under her arms brought on a tremble.

"Very well. Come to my desk."

Sheila followed the office manager, feeling like an errant school child.

When they got to the reception area, two men stood talking near the entrance doors—the guy with crinkly, near-black hair and another, much taller fellow with silver hair. They tipped their heads to Louise Hewett, who rolled her eyes and sat down as if gliding onto a throne.

After a minute scrutinizing each pathetic page, wearing the expression of a long-suffering martyr, she straightened the papers on her desk with a ker-plunk—ker-plunk—ker-plunk. Shaking her head like she truly never had seen such a disaster, she said, "Mrs. Gallagher, I'll call if you should come back."

Sheila passed the attorneys, her eyes on the tile floor, and pushed open one of the heavy doors. Outside huge raindrops hit her cheeks, and she had three miles to walk with no umbrella. More terrible than this, she had forgotten her purse in that dinky room. For a second she thought, *Just forget it.* She couldn't face those awful people again. But she remembered a twenty-dollar bill tucked in the zipper compartment. Enough to buy groceries for a week. *I won't cry.* She decided to go in and politely ask for her purse and then leave as fast as possible.

When she re-entered their reception area, the attorneys were laughing loudly as the office manager said, "...even in Minn – e – so – tah..."

Louise Hewett barely looked at Sheila, mumbling out her problem. Meanwhile the attorneys stared at her, seemingly in disbelief.

Returning, the office manager carried the purse between her fingers like a dead mouse being held by the tail. In the other hand she grasped the scrunched-up paper with Sheila's streaked fingerprints.

"On second thought, Mrs. Gallagher, you are not a good fit. Forget about a call." She raised her head to a loftier height. "Perhaps Douglas Aircraft is hiring."

Sheila took her purse, whispered thanks, and scurried from the office.

During the soaking walk home to the apartment, her tears mixed with the rain. At last she reached the building and trudged up the steps to her door, water sloshing in her sandals.

Rent wasn't due for over a week. Surely a job would materialize soon.

***

Sheila sobbed for a long time that night, lying in Jim's arms, saying between hiccups: "What am I going to do? I don't even know how to operate the stupid machines here in California"; then, "I've gotta find something—I can't go back"; then, "I'll die if I have another interview like that"; then, "It'll be okay. I know it'll be okay"; then, "Oh God. I feel sick. It's just like my father said."

Jim reassured her, "It'll be all right, my little doll." He brushed back her hair and kissed her forehead.

Next morning, before he left for the ship and another five days of maneuvers, he said, "You need to rest for a while. Why not take the day off?"

She didn't respond with her usual, It's time to grow up!

As awful as Sheila felt about not continuing the job search, she peered into the mirror at her blotchy skin and bloodshot eyes and tumbled back onto the Murphy bed. When she did arise, hours later, Jim was gone, and she mentally kicked herself for wasting so much time.

From the manager's apartment, she called to make another appointment with Mr. Bosanka. The receptionist set their fifth meeting for the next morning. Sheila cringed. What did Louise Hewett tell him after she finished laughing with Briggs and Newell?

***

As soon as she walked back to his desk, Sheila saw that Mr. Bosanka sat there beaming.

"You're in luck," he informed her. "You still haven't given me a phone number, otherwise I'd have called. Douglas started hiring sooner than expected."

For the rest of the week, she went through the testing, interviewing, and new employee indoctrination process. The men reminded her of Mr. Bosanka, and the women had unpolished, clipped fingernails and no scarves. After waiting in so many rooms and signing so many papers, including a security clearance that made her feel important, Sheila was told to report on Monday, August 2nd. She had a job typing change orders for the DC-10, from hard copies, not a Dictaphone, at a salary of $400 a month—quite a raise over her $315 at the bank in Minneapolis.

Jim's ship was still out, so she couldn't tell him. Instead she used the apartment manager's phone once more and called her parents.

Her father said, "Big deal. You've got a job. Doesn't mean a thing. You belong here at home with your mother." It was late in the day, but his words were as forceful as ever.

Her mother, vague from vodka, said something about, "Your father's right," when she took her turn to speak.

Sheila cut the conversation short. She thanked the apartment manager and said, "I'll get a phone first paycheck."

On the walk past closed doors of other apartments, on the way to her own, she repeated, "I will not...will not...will not go back to Minneapolis."

## SCRAGGLY NAILS

*The only inspiration for this story that I can recall has to do with the fingernails. Long ago, a friend of mine told me about a kind woman who showed her extra attention during a very difficult time of her life. My friend was a teenager and she had a habit of biting her fingernails. In addition to showing my friend loving attention, this older woman admired my friend's beautiful hands, gave her a manicure, and encouraged her to start caring for her fingernails. That imagery stuck in my mind and eventually set me off on this story.*

# Scraggly Nails

Published by *Cactus Heart*, Spring 2014

For six months my father, my brother, and I had been living in a cramped two-bedroom apartment near Northwest Electrical Engineering, the Seattle company that Dad had purchased the previous year. Even though he and Mom had been staunch supporters of John F. Kennedy, and as such brought Tim and me to several Democratic fund-raisers, Dad failed to vote that November.

It was now January, and I'd returned to my sixth-grade class, still "the new girl," after the most dismal of Christmases, with a wilted poinsettia plant as our only decoration.

Dad came back to the apartment one night at 5:00 instead of his usual 8:00 or 9:00.

I'd made Kraft macaroni and cheese with sliced-up hot dogs for dinner.

He shrugged out of his damp-from-the-rain overcoat, and ignoring my meal, said, "We're going to have a visitor next week...she's really special to me." This was the most excitement I'd heard in his voice since Mom got sick.

"She?" My older brother, Tim, with an abundance of girlfriends during his partying high school days, had told me, "Dad'll marry again before too long, Kelly." With our father's announcement, Tim narrowed his eyes, I'm sure considering whether Dad had already met a woman to replace our mother.

My chest tightened as I fought back an urge to gnaw at my fingernails—a new habit.

Dad used to bring spicy-smelling pink carnations to Mom before their occasional "date." I'd see her poring over a newspaper at the kitchen table, trying to decide what movie she wanted to see after they went to their favorite Italian restaurant. Later, I'd hear hushed giggles coming through their bedroom door. The next day, no matter how tired he was from work at his very own company, Dad would be right there next to Mom at my horseback-riding lessons, intensely watching me and Bo. Later, they'd give me pointers from what they'd seen.

"Mrs. O'Donnell is from Toronto—the widow of an old professor of mine," Dad filled us in. "I lived with them for a while, saving money to come to the States. She took care of my laundry, fed me, gave me advice. I liked her a whole lot better than him."

Once, when I was about nine, while hauling my saddle past his office alcove, I knocked over Dad's blue glass desk lamp. I watched that beautiful lamp as it shattered into a million pieces.

With a hurt tone, nothing like his normal measured voice, Dad said, "Mrs. O'Donnell gave me that."

Later, Mom told me, "Something special of your father's got ruined, and he doesn't care about treasures the way you and I do." She gave me a big hug, and continued, "I know you feel terrible. We'll look for something nice to replace it."

"She's going to be in Vancouver visiting family," Dad now went on. "Wants to see me and meet you two."

"To stay overnight?" No one had come to visit us in this apartment.

"She'll take the train to Seattle and I'll pick her up, then bring her back to the station next morning."

I figured Tim would be around for dinner, and then either meet up with his current honey or hang out in the bedroom he and Dad shared, watching their television. I planned to retreat to my own bedroom, but I was worried.

"Let's make something fancy," Dad said. "From one of Mom's recipes."

"Maybe we should bring in food." Tim mopped up the last of his orange cheese sauce with a piece of bread and popped his remaining hot-dog coin into his mouth.

"You're right. How about The Bells' pot roast?" We ordered food from this nearby café more nights than not. "Can you set a nice table, Kelly?"

This wouldn't be easy since Mom's china and crystal and silver had been sold, along with most everything else, in order to pay medical bills. "Sure, Dad." Then, trying to act casual, I said, "Where will she sleep?"

"Plenty of room in your bed."

Dad and Tim slept in my old twins, and I'd been given my parents' set with its queen. Dad had said, "I can buy you new furniture if this bothers you."

The way he said it, with a catch in his voice, I knew there wasn't an extra penny to cover the cost. "It'll be okay."

"You can have our television for your own," he added, as if offering this prize would make it easier. When I wasn't reading, I would watch any old program—even Lawrence Welk. So far, no friend from my new school had come for a spend-over. The way I felt all the time, like I didn't have the energy to crack a smile, acted the opposite of a magnet, pushing away anyone who tried to know me.

"You're going to like Mrs. O'Donnell. No one has ever been so kind to me…except, of course, your mother." His face brightened in a forgotten way. This was the first time he'd said anything about Mom since the funeral service. Dad had met her while she was living with an aunt, her only living relative, soon after he arrived in Seattle. He used to joke about how a fine beauty like her, personal secretary to the president of Northwest Electrical Engineering, took pity on a Newfie far away from home.

Dreading Mrs. O'Donnell's visit, I thought about going to stay at a friend's house in Woodinville, even though there'd been no contact with any of those old friends since our move. That way, she could have my bedroom to herself. But Dad had said Mrs. O'Donnell wanted to meet us. Besides, at the last 4-H meetings I attended, the mothers hovered over me as they passed out cookies, acting like if I just got enough sugar, everything in my life would be fantastic. I didn't want to go through that kind of attention again.

Pondering what to do about the troubling sleep arrangement, I momentarily considered using the front-room sofa, and she could have my bed, until I remembered we didn't have a sofa anymore. Dad's desk, with the replacement lamp—a pale imitation of the original—bookshelves, and an office chair, took up most of the room. A couple of tattered upholstered chairs filled the corner.

Our Woodinville house's new owners had expressed delight at buying most of the furnishings as well as Mom's knickknacks. They raved about her garden and the five acres where even our German shepherd Max, the cats, and my pony Bo Jangles were to remain.

Dad had told me, "You've outgrown Bo anyhow. We'll find a stable where you can ride a real horse." So far, this hadn't happened.

"How old is she?" I imagined Mrs. O'Donnell being a witch with hairs sprouting from the mole on her nose.

"About sixty when I lived with them. Must be over eighty. Amazing. A woman that age coming all the way from Toronto."

During her cancer, before she went to the hospital for good, Mom had stayed home in the very bed that later became mine. What if Mrs. O'Donnell died in her sleep? With me alongside of her?

That night, I stared at the ceiling, which I did every other night, this time wondering where else I could go during her visit. The clock said 1:30 when I scooped up my pillow and blanket. Passing Dad and Tim's room, I stopped and listened to their duet of snores. Once in the bathroom, I wrapped the blanket around my shivering body and hugged the pillow close to my chest. I could curl, snail-like, in the tub, even if the shower curtain did smell of mildew. Then I thought, what if she needs to come in here? Don't old people go to the toilet a lot at night? At least my grandma and grandpa did.

I stumbled into the front room, with stains from previous tenants on its carpet. Could I camp out beneath the kitchen table? When I was little, I'd made a tent and crept beneath it and read to my teddy bear with Mom's flashlight. On all fours, ignoring crusty spots, I crawled under the table, rolled up in my blanket, and bunched my pillow into a mound. Every time I shifted, my knees bumped against a wooden leg. After about half an hour, I fumbled my way out and looked around.

Neither of the upholstered chairs looked comfortable, but if I pushed them together, edge to edge, they formed a cot of sorts. Satisfied that this was the best solution, I bundled up in my blanket and snuggled into a ball, trying it out for size. Not bad. I decided to sneak off here when she visited, and leave a sleeping Mrs. O'Donnell all to herself.

For the next few evenings, Dad talked about her, saying things like: "She helped many students who found themselves short of cash," and "Didn't have any children of her own," and "She took me to the airport…told me that I was doing exactly the right thing moving to the States and taking a position with Northwest."

Dad's family still lived "around the bay" in Newfoundland. When Mom was alive, we traveled back there every few years, but none of those relatives, and there were many, had ever been anywhere except St. John's, and couldn't figure out why Dad had left. Not one of them reminded me of him. I baked sugar cookies and decorated them with Grandma, and would tag along with Grandpa, checking in on all his buddies, me chewing on a piece of his Juicy Fruit gum while they sipped their brews.

At this time, I didn't know when we'd ever go to Newfoundland again.

***

This woman, with fine lines that barely showed on her sculpted face, had sparkling silver strands woven through butter-yellow hair. Aquamarine eyes, like Mom's birthstone ring, were emphasized by golden skin, the kind that looks lightly tanned year-round.

She held out a hand to me. It felt small and delicate in my own. As she drew away, I noticed a slight scrape. Her fingernails were oval and painted pale petal pink.

"The Christmas-card photos didn't do justice to your good-looking children, Carl." She smiled at me. "You must take after your mother, with that thick, dark hair and those big brown eyes."

During the presidential campaign, I'd wondered if Mom, whose cheeks no longer flushed with pleasure but rather were sunken and pale, had been as lovely as pregnant Jackie when she was expecting me.

Mrs. O'Donnell turned to Tim. "You're so much like your father at this age. Every bit as tall."

Tim showed more interest in her than I would have expected, uncharacteristically cutting a phone conversation short. During our meal, he asked many questions about the professor, and finally said, "I want to be an engineer." This was news to me. Hanging out with his girlfriend-of-the-moment seemed to be all he ever thought about. Dad also registered surprise, sitting straighter in his chair and focusing on my brother. Continuing with the memories, Mrs. O'Donnell said to Dad, "You were always a favorite of George's."

"I never realized that." Dad shifted his attention to her.

"He was a hard one to know—like many engineers, so immersed in his work that he seldom showed his feelings. Still, he often praised you as the best student he'd seen in years."

By dessert, which was raspberry sherbet, Mrs. O'Donnell said, "How about you, Kelly, what are your interests?"

"Reading, I guess."

"What do you like to read?"

"Anything to do with horses."

"I used to ride. Have you ever had one of your own?"

"A pony. He's at home."

"Maybe someday you'll have another."

"Maybe…"

"What about your 4-H? It was mentioned often in Christmas letters."

"I don't participate anymore."

She paused, maybe not knowing what else to say, then turned back to Dad and Tim.

This was fine with me. Picking at my scraggly nails, I waited until enough time had passed so that I could go to my room. As it turned out, Tim stayed with them, asking more questions about engineering. I left my door open, so Mrs. O'Donnell wouldn't have to knock, and thought about watching my television, but decided to read My Friend Flicka for about the fifth time instead.

Upon hearing them make good-night sounds, I shut my light off and turned toward the wall, wanting her to find me "asleep" when she crawled in. I dozed a bit while she used the bathroom, yet the minute my mattress moved with weight from her body, I became alert, like Bo when he sniffed something new in the air.

"Are you awake?" she whispered.

I didn't say a thing, keeping my eyes tightly closed, but smelling her faintly sweet night cream. She rolled away from me, and after a short while her breath came evenly. I hoped it wouldn't stop before my escape. She might be different from the witch I'd envisioned; still, she was ancient. Up close, her neck sagged into deep lines, and her hands that had felt so delicate, despite the well-groomed nails and polish, looked twisted and lumpy, like claws.

Several long minutes passed while I waited to make sure she was sound asleep before I quietly stole out to the front room.

The chairs-made-into-a-cot proved to be less than adequate. As I thrashed around, they slid apart, dumping my rear on the floor. I stood three times to shove them back together. Eventually, I sat up in one chair, chewing at my nails and picturing our old house, imagining someone else sleeping in my room, fretting about my pets getting attached to the new kids. My mind was so busy reliving a gallop with Bo, Max running along next to us, happily barking, that I didn't hear her come in.

"Hard night?"

Huddled there with my eyes wide open, I couldn't pretend. "Can't sleep."

"Would you like some cocoa?"

At least we had milk and Hershey's syrup in the refrigerator. "That'd taste good."

We sat together at the table with only Dad's desk lamp on for illumination, drinking our cocoa, talking about my new school.

"Have you made any friends?"

"Nope."

"Sometimes it takes a while."

"There are some nice girls...it's me."

"When I was your age, my mother got sick."

"Did she die?"

"Not right away, but she endured so much pain it was as if she'd left me."

I didn't know anyone else who had lost a mother. "My mom was sick for all of fifth grade," I said. "One day she drove me to a 4-H meeting and everything seemed normal, and the next day she didn't even look like herself."

"Everything about my mother changed too." The desk lamp flickered. "She became this wasted-away person with hollow eyes and shrunken skin."

"I didn't want to be in the same room with her." I'd never said anything like this to anyone.

"It was hard to kiss her cheek. There was a smell—like a soggy, forgotten garden—the smell of death, I've come to realize. At the end, her hands continually smoothed the silky top of a blanket. I wanted to say 'Be still!' And then she was."

"How long did it take for you to quit feeling bad?"

"I still mourn for her, but I quit feeling ashamed. I was a child and I'd never been around anyone who died."

We sipped our cocoa for several quiet moments.

"I miss her so much…the way she used to be." It felt sad, but also good to say it.

Mrs. O'Donnell reached out and took my hand. In a minute or so, she started to examine my messed-up fingernails. "Tomorrow, I'm going to give you a manicure, and I'll leave my polish here." Her aquamarine eyes glistened as she went on. "It's late. Please come to your room. I promise…I won't die tonight."

"How'd you know?"

"I would've felt exactly the same way."

***

She rubbed my back with her twisted, lumpy hands, and for the first time since we'd moved to this apartment, the bed didn't seem haunted. Soon my body relaxed, my breathing evened, and I drifted off.

# THE OLDEST RESORT

*I went on a weekend similar to the one at the old hotel in Tokeland, Washington that is described in the story. The characters are all imaginary, as are the situations and incidents. However, we did discover preparations for a wedding reception in the hotel's main room and laughed at its simplicity. We left the hotel for dinner and an evening of music in the town. By the time we got back the reception was over and the main room was cleared up. We did party into the early morning hours entirely too loudly, thinking we had the place to ourselves. We didn't know that the honeymooners were staying right across the hall from the room where we gathered. If we had known, would we have toned down our own fun? I hope so. In the middle of the night the young couple snuck out in the way of the couple in my story. I always felt badly about this. Hence, the inspiration for this story.*

# The Oldest Resort

Published by *Blue Lake Review*, July 2014

Francie's apartment on Capitol Hill is ten long miles from Brian's West Seattle waterfront condo. The big question: When will he ask her to move in? She's started packing.

Snuggled on his hunter green leather sofa, pretending to watch the second game of the World Series, she opens her eyes wide, forcing herself awake. Brian tips and settles his Dodgers cap, absorbed in the action. Finally, seventh inning, a break while the crowd sings "Take Me Out to the Ballgame."

Nuzzling her neck, Brian whispers, "How'd I get so lucky to find you?"

"Beats me." Francie almost says, If you're so lucky, how come we're not living together? In another month his divorce finalizes. Will that get the ball rolling?

Cousin Lisa has been "shacked up," as Francie's father calls it, for almost a year. It's 1978. This happens! Still, Francie's stomach clenches. The staunch Catholic Shaughnessys all but ostracized Aunt Lorraine every time she, in her words, pulled a "shenanigan." Now, shaking their heads, they repeat, "Cousin Lisa's on the same track. Like mother, like daughter."

Speculating about the family's reaction to her behavior, Francie blushes recalling last night in Brian's water bed, him mumbling, "Good to be with someone who likes it."

Was Suzanne cold and unaffectionate? With remarks like this, she has pieced together an idea of Brian's marriage.

After the game ends, Francie and Brian stand, elbows propped on the railing of his deck, watching a ferry make its way toward Seattle. "The guys are planning a party weekend. You'll go with me, right?" His even features lift expectantly.

Francie straightens. "Where?" Dinner and a movie with his friends—fine—but two whole days?

"Todd Caldwell, you haven't met him, a FIJI." All Brian's friends are frat brothers. "He bought a hotel near Westport in a place called, get this, Tokeland. It's the oldest resort in Washington. We're having a bash before Todd starts the remodel." Brian's dark eyebrows scrunch together. "He left his father's law practice and Georgie quit selling pharmaceuticals so they could do this together." Brian works for his father's construction company.

"Georgie?"

"Todd's wife, Georgia McBride...McBride Drugs was owned by her family." Walgreens has recently bought out this local chain.

Brian studies Francie. "You okay about the weekend?"

"As long as I'm with you, I'll have fun," she says. Gray clouds are blowing in from the south. At a distance, the inbound ferry and the outbound ferry meet.

"Great! These guys are like family." Brian doesn't have any siblings. "We can stop in Hoquiam on the way back so you can introduce me to your parents."

"Good idea." Hoquiam is the last place Francie wants to bring him. Not until they're on more solid ground. But, what can she say? My parents are on a round-the-world cruise? They never travel.

"Better go." Brian puts his hand on her waist, meaning head for the bedroom. "Or you'll get back to the apartment way too late."

Again! Francie shivers with the first drops of rain.

***

On a recent visit home, her sister, Colleen, like a child wishing to be a princess, said, "Strange outfit but it sure looks cute."

In Annie Hall baggy pants, suspenders, man's shirt, and vest, Francie posed, before taking off her slouch hat and giving a little twirl. Thanks to her Nordstrom employee discount, she stays in style.

"You can get away with it, flashing those dimples and big smile." A wistful pause before Colleen said, "I ran into Darrell. He asked for you...hasn't married yet."

"He'll make someone very happy." Darrell, with his dirty-blond hair cut in a mullet like every other guy in town, has earnest, blue eyes that show a girl he'll never treat her wrong.

"He's a manager at the mill."

"No surprise." The Hoquiam Monster, mouth agape, lurked in a corner of Francie's mind.

***

Next morning, after a mere three hours sleep in her own bed, Francie goes through the motions at work, trying not to nod off. Everything is falling into place. First, her promotion to accountant. Then, meeting Brian.

One lunch hour, shortly after recovering from a virus that almost forced her to move back home, she was in the men's department choosing a Father's Day gift. Someone nudged her and a male voice said, "Which do you like?"

Francie turned, expecting to see Jeremy, the only salesman working. Instead, she stared at one of the Italian silk ties she'd dismissed as too expensive and something Dad would only wear to weddings and funerals, lying against a broad chest that sure didn't belong to skinny Jeremy. Crinkly, brown eyes and thick, brown hair, neatly trimmed, filled in her first impression of Brian Willard. He held a green polo shirt in one hand and a blue in the other. Francie pointed to the green.

***

Her father has a head like Khrushchev's and a temperament to match. She absolutely does not want to marry a bald man, even though they're supposed to be super virile. Francie can't imagine that with her parents. Maybe thirty years ago before Mom drooped on every square inch of her body and developed a disposition to match. When she used to bring up the idea of a job, Dad would say, "I want my wife right here.

Don't want to go looking for her every time I need a button sewed on or my pants pressed." As a logger, he didn't have a lot of call for pressed pants. At barely twenty-six, Colleen lives in Hoquiam with three children and another on the way. Her husband works at the mill. To Francie, the town has become a hungry ocean creature waiting to swallow her alive.

***

Friday the thirteenth, in the dark, they arrive at the Tokeland Hotel. "Good thing you're not superstitious," Brian had said. He didn't know that even making love outside the Sacrament of Marriage could summon up horrific images. As they pull onto the dirt parking strip, Brian expertly maneuvers his green Z-car into place. Francie notices three late-model vehicles in a scraggly row.

Brian pushes open the ripped screen door, which squeaks like a mouse, and strides to the scratched oak counter, where he dings a tarnished bell several times. When no one appears he hits it a few more times. A dusty smell, like the attic at home, makes Francie stifle a sneeze as she checks for rodents scurrying past her platform shoes.

"All right already, I'm coming," a male voice hollers. Moments later, a big, overall-clad guy bounds in, thunks a wrench onto the counter, and spreads his hands across the wood. "Fixing a leak." He grins.

"Franceen, the lummox with the tool is Todd, owner of this fine hotel, and a sometimes buddy of mine."

"We're always tight." Todd takes in Francie's outfit, the same one her sister recently admired. "Here, you can stick this in a pocket of those baggy pants." He slides the wrench toward her.

"She looks cute." Brian squeezes her shoulder.

"Just kidding. C'mon, everybody's waiting."

Traipsing up the steps and down a dark corridor, ancient floorboards groan accompanied by a distant rock song and faraway voices. They pass several shut doors, aiming for a stream of light at the end of the corridor. Getting closer, Francie picks out words.

"…hell are they?" a male says.

"I told Brian as soon after six as possible," a female says.

"Probably stopped off at his place for a little party of their own."

"Oh Aaron, shhh." Then, stage-whispered, "She's...interesting. Do you suppose Brian's found the one."

"Tricia! You be quiet too," says another female.

Francie stiffens, clutching Brian's hand.

"Bunch of jerks." He laughs.

She follows him into the room, worrying that despite the "cute" remark, her clothes are all wrong. The three other girls wear jeans and sweatshirts. Francie slips off her shoes and hat.

"Where ya been?" demands Charlie Moorhead, a guy with wire-framed glasses who works at his father's stock brokerage. He often comments that since becoming a father he has to settle down. The baby was left with his parents so he and his wife, Kelly, could have this getaway.

Brian makes an excuse about heavy traffic. He withholds that they did stop at his condo.

An hour later, in what will be their room for the weekend, Charlie and Kelly, still wearing what looks like a maternity top, lean against each other on an iron bed amid a rumple of worn, pink chenille. Everyone else is plopped on battered kitchen chairs or sprawled on the floor. Another joint's glow circles the room. Open coolers with beer and wine and Dreamsicles sit in a corner, with chips and pretzels nearby. Brian and Francie didn't take time for dinner, but the loud radio camouflages her rumbling stomach.

"Remember that funky place on Rosarita Beach—spring break— sophomore year?" Brian starts another story. "We dragged booze in right under the manager's nose."

"Charlie almost drowned," says Aaron Petrie. He wears a Yankees cap. Since they entered the room, he's been rubbing in their win to Brian. Acting nonchalant, he's also spoken about being "between engagements," living off a trust fund.

"Never bodysurfed again." Charlie winces.

"The undertow almost carried him away," says Georgie. She's playing hostess to Todd's host, both of them replenishing snacks. Her apple-patterned apron is similar to the ones Francie's mother dons when cooking huge family dinners.

After they continue with about the twentieth shared memory, Kelly, who once must have been shapely but still carries extra weight after the baby's birth, says, "Franceen, are you bored to tears?"

"Not at all. It's interesting." With no sorority sisters or adventures backpacking through Europe, she listens to how people who didn't work two jobs in order to put themselves through college lived. Occasionally, she drops in a remark about her own background, something they find amusing, especially as the evening progresses and everyone gets more high. Besides a couple of light tokes, to not draw attention, Francie has refrained, staying as clearheaded as she tries to be when working on balance sheets. Looking toward Charlie and Kelly, she remarks, "That whole setup—bedstead, bedspread—looks like my parents'."

"Your mother and father sleep in something like that?" Tricia Petrie tucks her pointed chin.

"Just like it. Back in Hoquiam."

"Hoq…what a hoot, Hoq…Hoq…," Charlie says.

"It's Ho-qui-am, dummy," Kelly says. "You're cut off." Then, she holds the roach clip to his lips. "I wish you would've been with us for those times, Franceen."

She doesn't say, You're more fun than Suzanne, but Francie's sure that's what she means.

Encouraged, she continues to regale them with family tidbits.

"Your aunt actually did it with the landlord in order to get a new refrigerator?" Tricia jerks up like a marionette.

"Town gossip says she'd fuck anybody to get what she wanted." Francie nearly chokes on the word she never uses.

"Ohhh…." Tricia slumps.

Georgie, Kelly, and Tricia wear expressions of fatigued disbelief. The guys are beyond caring, but the girls find Francie as fascinating as a sea serpent dropped into their midst.

About 3:00 a.m., the other couples leave Charlie and Kelly's room, straggling off to bed. Kelly twiddles her pointer finger "good-bye" through a crack in their wall, bringing on last giggles as the girls trip on by.

Brian and Francie's room doesn't have any holes in the walls, but the bed is so broken down that she dozes mid-valley. He sacks out in a sleeping bag beside their door.

They get up early, stiff-limbed. The guys speed through showers and give a moldy-smelling communal bathroom over to the girls for scrubbing and primping. After a quick rinse in icy water, Francie puts on a T-shirt and cutoffs. Dishes clatter downstairs, and a crash sounds like logs falling. Shortly, a tap on the door startles her dabbing lipstick in front of a mirror that makes her brown eyes look right out of a Picasso. She turns the tarnished brass knob to check. Each guy holds a mug of coffee. Brian kisses the top of her head before handing over one.

"God, do I need this," Georgie takes several gulps.

"Me too." Francie takes a sip, hating the taste.

Squinting above her steaming mug at the rusted fixtures and stained walls, Tricia, a part-time employee at her mother's furnishings boutique, says, "This reminds me of bathrooms in the dorms." She crinkles her narrow nose.

Francie lived in the U's dorms for two years before moving to an apartment with five other girls. "There's only one bathroom at home." She pauses for effect. "With my sister and me and Mom and Dad and lots of visiting family to use it. This wallpaper may even have the same shell design." She scratches her fingernail over a peeling strip. The pale-pink polish still looks fresh.

"That must have been hard." Kelly frowns.

Georgie and Tricia look stone-faced. This sort of banter played well with everyone high. Not so, in the bright light of morning, with all of them bummed out.

Todd and Georgie, wearing her apple-patterned apron, serve pancakes. They again apologize for the state of the place, and together say, "Wait'll next time."

Goose bumps cover Francie's bare arms. Looking at the stacked logs in the fireplace, she wishes someone would light them.

"I hope you don't change too much. It's charming, and Franceen feels right at home here," Tricia says.

Brian pulls Francie, relieved as a tadpole darting into protective weeds, close against his chest.

"How kind of you to think of that, Pa-tree-sha," Kelly says.

While the others drink second and third mugfuls of coffee, plans are made to explore Tokeland. Francie doesn't say that shirttail relations, who refer to Hoquiam as "the big city," live close by.

"I got a net and volleyball in my trunk," Aaron says. "We can play and listen to the Yankees win again." He picks up the radio.

"No way," Brian says.

Everyone agrees that the deserted beach, even though it's overrun with clumps of grass, sounds like a great idea. The golden autumn day, with a smell of ocean in the air, makes them want to stay outside.

Once set up, Aaron, repeatedly throws the ball and catches it, before saying, "We could use a couple of girls."

Tricia says, "You've got to be kidding."

Kelly offers, "Maybe working up a sweat will chisel off a pound or two of this baby fat."

Georgie, after looking toward Francie, says, "What the heck. I can play. Our picnic is ready to go."

Francie could have volunteered. She used to be pretty good. Instead, she chooses to listen to Tricia's chatter rather than self-consciously stumbling around. Ten minutes into her monologue, with hoots and hollers from players in the background, and Francie yearns for a book. Tricia goes on about another Theta married to a politician in California. After thoroughly exhausting this subject, she says, "Does Brian hear anything from Suzanne?"

Surprised, Francie says, "He never talks about her."

"She was my roommate at The House. Don't know why I care. Poor Brian. Such a bitch!"

"In what way?"

"Had an affair with his boss." A smug smile tightens her mouth. "They're getting married in a few months,"

"His boss?"

"That's why Brian left the bank. Suzanne's still there. He'd become a vice president too. Last thing he wanted to do was go back to work for his dad. Hasn't he told you any of this?"

Francie shrugs, taken aback at such a horrible aspect of his marriage, and it's news to her that he doesn't like working for Willard Construction. The company has almost completed another office building on Third. She thought he was excited about it.

"He's ready to move on," Tricia continues. "You're nicer than Suzanne, and Brian looks a whole lot happier." Apparently done with gathering information, she hollers, "Hey Georgie, isn't it time for lunch?"

Francie wishes for this part of the conversation to go on, but Georgie starts to divvy up sandwiches.

In the late afternoon, they head back. Todd says he can't cook dinner because a wedding party has reserved the hotel's main room.

"A reception? Here?" Tricia grimaces.

Todd and Georgie exchange annoyed glances.

"Maybe this is a special place for them. It's got a lot of character," Kelly says.

When they enter the main room, leaving a trail of sand, Francie sees a table smack in the middle of the cracked linoleum floor. A small wedding cake perches atop, with paper plates, plastic forks, and napkins that look like they came from a metal dispenser spread around it. Lumpy, threadbare sofas and dilapidated rockers have been shoved against the walls. The fireplace, still set to be lit, feels drafty and has the acrid smell of old smoke.

Tricia says, "We should have a mock wedding."

All of a sudden, no one but Francie seems tired.

"You be the bride," Tricia points, "and Brian can be the groom since you two aren't married." She mouths the word yet, rolling her eyes.

"What d'ya think?" Brian says.

"I don't care." Maybe this will give him some ideas.

They line up around the cake. Charlie holds an old logging manual open, like a minister officiating. Behind Brian stands Aaron holding a broom like a shotgun, a scowl on his sunburned face. Rather than doing a fake read, Charlie leers over his wire frames at Francie's T-shirt-covered chest. She thrusts it out for the camera in Kelly's hands. If they want to play this game, she'll give them a laugh. Their fun lasts for several minutes before boredom sets in and they all lumber back to the rooms. Francie fixes the tipped plastic figures on the cake before leaving.

That night they drive to a nearby steak house. Georgie says, "This spot hasn't heard of medium rare, and most of the locals dump A.1. all over their meat, but we can request it cooked the way we want." After dinner and dancing to music from the fifties, Todd gives Brian a ring of keys. "Make sure everything is locked up tomorrow when you leave." After that, he and Georgie take off for Seattle to talk to their parents about further financing.

The shadowed hotel looks solemn when the group returns. A dirty old pickup, that no one but Francie seems to see, has been parked over to the side in order to give their cars plenty of room. The cake and table have disappeared and the main-room furniture shoved back in place. Last flickers of a fire remain. They move on to Charlie and Kelly's room, where again they play loud music while everyone talks and laughs and smokes and drinks. Going strong after 3:00 a.m., Charlie says, "This can't end!" Early tomorrow it will be back to Seattle and grown-up lives.

In the midst of Aaron's next dirty joke, "Then a logger...," the door across the hall clicks open. A young man and an obviously pregnant young woman duck out. The fellow, in a red plaid wool jacket, smiles uncertainly, sort of an acknowledgment. The young woman burrows her face into his arm as they slink away, his boots clunking.

"The newlyweds!" Brian says. "Todd didn't mention they were staying."

"Who would've thought they'd spend their first night at the Tokeland Hotel." Tricia yawns.

"Where will they go?" Kelly says.

Francie doesn't tell them that, from a glimpse, the groom's ruddy face reminded her of Great Uncle Rudy.

Sheepishly, Charlie says, "I think it's time we all go to bed."

Brian's last words from his sleeping bag are, "I wish we could think of some way to make it up.... I'll send a check.... Todd can give it to them."

"Sure," Francie murmurs to his back. "A check."

***

The rest of the night, she listens to Brian's even breathing. With illumination coming in through cracks around the door, she stares, wide-eyed in the gloom, at the many-times-patched ceiling, recalling other patched ceilings.

She's first one in the bathroom next morning, getting ready to go. During the drive, she stays quiet. Brian carries on about the Series and his frustration with the Dodgers, and then asks, "Are you feeling all right?"

"Tired."

"Understandable. We'll skip stopping by your parents' place this time, and get you back to my bed." He reaches over and rubs her inner thigh. "You have to start staying all the time."

Passed muster with his friends, Francie thinks.

When she doesn't say anything, he says, "You know...move in."

"Let's talk about it later. I need a night, alone, at my apartment."

"Okay. And about your parents...I'll be moving down to Tokeland in the next month. Going into partnership with Todd and Georgie. So, after we get married you'll be over this way all the time."

Francie squints her eyes and leans her head against the seat, as the Hoquiam Monster slides closer, wearing a smirk on its slimy face.

## SECOND THOUGHTS

*Several years ago my husband and I took an anniversary trip to Kauai, our favorite Hawaiian island. The condo we stayed at was spacious and well-appointed. When we first walked in and looked at the fantastic view we were confident that the right lodging situation had been chosen. That night we went out to dinner and came back and went to bed early in preparation for lots of fun activities the next day. It was then that I became fully aware of the crashing waves hitting against cliffs that had looked so spectacular earlier. For some reason this noise, much like a semi-truck hitting into a cement wall, didn't bother my husband. My sleep, however, was disturbed for the whole trip. I wandered the condo, looking for anywhere to doze off in order to get away from the infernal noise. This became the inspiration for my story, "Second Thoughts." My protagonist is miserable in his relationship and the racket, accompanied with lack of sleep, almost causes him to do something he will regret. Ultimately, he makes a decision about the unhappy relationship.*

# Second Thoughts

Published by *Imitation Fruit*, September 2014

Once this small gray creature dashed in front of my car. A squirrel. My brakes screeched as I saved the little fellow, but got rear-ended in the process; fortunately, with no injuries to anyone, including that squirrel. It's said that everyone has the capacity for killing, when pushed to the limit by someone or something. Murder had never entered my mind, even when my wife left me for Brad Gilman, a math teacher at one of Seattle's middle schools, where she taught science. A few years ago, they developed a team approach with their classes, and frequent late-night planning sessions began to cover more than curriculum.

Leslie gave me blond-haired, cherub-faced twin girls who resembled her. They were ten years old, and our divorce allowed for visits every weekend, as well as some holidays. At our final settlement appointment, she said, "You're the best father ever, Hank. So much better than your own."

Leslie knew about my deceased dad's rages and clenched fist that always found its mark, tirades that escalated after my invalid mother died when I was twelve. Leslie used to hug me, her soft cheeks wet with tears, as she hesitantly tried to talk to me about my parents.

At this appointment, she added, "I don't want to deprive Sadie and Sally of any time they can have with you."

"It's appreciated." I knew she meant every word.

The attorney folded his hands on his desk and said, "I wish everyone could be this civil."

We exchanged tight-lipped smiles, certainly civil, while the room seemed to hum in harmony, like one of those sweet, old-time religion songs.

During the first months on my own, I never dated. Leslie kept our Dutch Colonial on Queen Anne Hill, and I purchased a two-bedroom house on prime property overlooking the city, with plenty of room for the girls and not too far from their friends. All the extra time made me work harder than ever as a financial planner. Since the early lean years, money hadn't been an issue, and by now, I made plenty with nowhere to spend it.

I should have known that an encounter with Gloria might occur at the Pike Place Market. Our breakup had been twelve years before, with only a few awkward chance meetings, and I really wasn't thinking about her as I spent at least half an hour wandering around the flower stalls, looking for a bouquet to give my assistant. When I finally turned from paying, a wrapped cone of lilies and roses in my hand, this wave of unexplained disappointment swept over me, as if I'd been pulled into an undertow.

Then, I heard a voice, a bit shrill. "Hank Porter! What are you doing here?"

The undertow rapidly dissipated. "Gloria. You still have the flower shop?"

"Sure do. It's flourishing."

"And you still pick up some of your blossoms here?"

"Every few days Are those for your wife? Her birthday? Making up?"

"Secretary's Day."

"Of course. I've sold quite a few arrangements." Gloria's shop filled one corner of the lobby in an office building a few blocks from the market. "Are you all right?" Her glittering brown eyes squeezed together in scrutiny.

Obviously, she'd taken note of my weight loss, pounds I could ill afford to lose. "I'm doing okay...Leslie and I have divorced."

She soaked in this information. "I should say I'm sorry, but that'd be a lie." She gave an unrepentant chuckle. "Not right. I am sorry. For you."

Gloria didn't say *not for that bitch*, but I mentally supplied the words.

We dated while I attended graduate school at the University of Washington. She'd refused to live together, but we saw each other every evening, until I met Leslie, who was my assistant at Robinson Rodgers Investments, working there until completion of a teaching certification. It was my first position, and I planned to buy an engagement ring for Gloria once I'd stashed away a few paychecks. But, something clicked with Leslie. Maybe it was her reserved manner and quiet concern. Soon, seeing each other at work wasn't enough. She would timidly coax me into conversation at Marco's Happy Hour. Before long, I began to cancel dates with Gloria, and then (hardest thing I've ever done), I told her it wasn't going to work.

On one of our many walks along Seattle's waterfront, she asked, "Is there someone else?"

I lied. "No. I need some space to concentrate on building my client list."

"Space? Fine. I'll give you space. But don't take too long." The implication was clear. She wouldn't wait.

When an announcement of Leslie's and my engagement hit the newspaper a short while later, Gloria sent a note with a bouquet of snapdragons "for the bride." In addition, it said, "Congratulations. Your business must be doing well."

I stuffed those flowers in my wastebasket.

Now, standing by her suppliers, I said, "How about you? Married? Kids?" Gloria's striking, pointy features hadn't mellowed.

"No on both counts."

Upon my return to the office, I gave the lilies and roses to my present, appreciative assistant, told her I was cutting out early, and met Gloria for wine.

Thus, our romance resurfaced.

At first, she wanted to be included in every weekend with the girls: soccer games, helping me chaperone their pizza party for a group of giggling fifth graders, sewing Halloween costumes. Sadie went as a mermaid. Sally went as a seahorse.

On a day when it was only the girls and me for a change, they said, in unison, "She sounds like a screeching crow." Covering their ears, each made squawking sounds.

"Be nice. Gloria has been good to you," I said, assuming, *They're jealous of anyone else in my life.*

Nothing had changed from earlier times. Gloria again refused to move in with me, so too soon we had a simple wedding ceremony at the courthouse, followed by a week in Vancouver.

The first part of November, she waited in the front seat of my new Mercedes while I dropped the girls off at my former home. Brad's Honda Civic sat in the driveway where I used to park in between weekend errands. When he answered the door with that smug expression on his ferret-face, I gave Sadie and Sally each a big hug (they tussled over who could make it last the longest) and returned to my car, barely acknowledging him.

After several minutes driving I told Gloria, "The girls don't have a soccer match next..."

"That's a relief. I've about had it with the cheerleading." She laughed.

*How would she take the news about Christmas?* My shoulders tensely inched toward my ears as I decided, *Another trip might be a good idea.* "Do you want to go somewhere over Thanksgiving?"

"Kauai would be fantastic. I've never been there. All the gardens."

"Oh...sure...Kauai." I'd gone there many times, to stay at Leslie's parents' place near Poipu Beach.

Fortunately, the condo Gloria located was at Princeville, a half an island away.

"It's above Honu Cove. Home of the green turtles," she told me. "Your kind of spot." She often teased that I pulled back from any kind of controversy or conflict or even discussion, like a turtle retreating into its shell.

Naturally, these comments reminded me of what went wrong all those years ago. Gloria continually demanded more communication, while Leslie made me feel comfortable.

That was one of the things, however, that Leslie said when we split up. "Brad brings me out of myself. You never could do that, Hank. Maybe you'll find someone who'll do the same for you."

Ah, Gloria.

Literature emailed by the real estate agency never mentioned how noisy this condo could be. It said: "The most spectacular view in Kauai." "Home of the green turtles." "Exquisitely appointed units."

We both gasped upon entering the living room, struck by magnificence framed in a high-ceilinged wall of windows. Cliffs plummeted hundreds of feet, with enormous waves below intermittently filling carved-out rock depressions the size of Olympic swimming pools. This spectacle, a few steps from our patio, stunned me into thinking, *Maybe this won't be so bad after all.*

That night, after her idea of an extremely sexy encounter, starting out in a see-through red getup, Gloria lay in dreamland next to me. The infernal racket, like semi-trucks crashing into cement walls, didn't bother her in the least. At last, I stumbled out of bed and commenced my roaming of the condo, searching for anywhere to find some peace.

We'd been at Honu Cove for three long days visiting every garden the island had to offer, and for me, three longer sleepless nights. So far, Gloria's harping caused me to retreat even further into myself, and now she'd insisted on a midnight walk. "To relax you."

Windows were dark in other condos. No one else seemed to have trouble sleeping.

"Isn't this wonderful?" She grabbed my arm and nuzzled against my skin.

I walked along next to her, tolerating that cheek rubbing against me, bringing out prickles in the balmy air.

"Nice." If I disagreed, said I wanted to go back to the condo, her voice would shift from its silky tone to a strident one, like a Brillo pad scraping out my ears. *You never want to do anything I want to do.*

Carefully stepping along the path, she said, "Aren't you glad we're here all by ourselves?"

"There's plenty of room in the condo for the girls," I couldn't help but say.

"There'd be no privacy."

I didn't want privacy. I wanted their skinny arms wrapped around my neck. Leslie and I used to each hold one when they were babies, bouncing in the waves at Poipu, the music of their giggles and our laughter in my ears. When they were toddlers, we strapped them into back carriers and hiked the Na Pali Trail. Our last trip together, we took turns sitting with one or the other on boat and helicopter rides. Did Brad, her new husband, the one who broke up our family, fill in for me?

"Remember our old strolls along Seattle's waterfront? We haven't done that this time. Only me, by myself, around our neighborhood." She lowered her voice to a whisper. "Sure not as romantic as here."

"No chaotic noise either."

"Oh, come on. It's rhythmical."

"Yeah, rhythms." My heart pounded like a kettledrum in an orchestra's back row.

"I've been thinking about Christmas. I want you to help me with decorating. There are boxes full of ornaments." She'd completely filled my organized storage space with a glut of her belongings.

"I'm going to have the girls at Christmas." I yanked at my T-shirt collar. "They can help decorate."

"What do you mean?"

"Leslie and Brad are coming to Kauai for a belated honeymoon. I'll have the girls. For two weeks."

"They can stay with us. They can help decorate. But, two whole weeks...I don't think so." Gloria shook her head.

"Where else can they go?"

"How 'bout staying with Leslie's parents? This is our first Christmas together, Hank. It's not fair."

Since we've married, the girls don't say mean things about Gloria's voice anymore, perhaps resigned to her presence. By this time, I heard exactly what they meant.

"They'll be back before New Year's."

"I don't want to wait 'til New Year's. I want you helping with the tree, putting up the lights, listening to the music, and being with me."

I stretched to my full six-foot-two. "I need to do this for my girls."

"It's always the girls with you!"

A one-foot fence, wooden poles with a rope looping between them, acted as a barrier between the path we were on and the cliff's edge. She walked closest to this fence, her fingers pressing deeply into my arm, the red fingernails feeling like they might draw blood.

"I'm their father, for God's sake."

"It doesn't have to be this way. You're obsessed with them."

*If she doesn't shut up, if these waves don't silence, if I can't get some sleep.* I gave a shove to her arm.

She skittered across the fence, onto the three-foot strip of lawn between her and a plunge into blackness. "Hey, be careful!"

"Sorry. I tripped."

"You better get some rest tonight. You're punchy."

*What did I almost do?* I wanted her gone. To get her voice out of my head. I swayed with the thunderous waves for several moments before, "I'm leaving."

"Going back to the condo?"

"No. Tomorrow. I'm leaving for Seattle."

"Are you sick?"

"I need to go." I didn't say, *I'm sick to death of you.*

"What am I supposed to do? It's Thanksgiving in two days!"

"Stay here, use the rental car, come back as planned."

"I can't make sense of this."

"Do I have to spell it out? We're done, Gloria. I want you out of my place immediately." *I'd rather be alone in my little house than end up in a prison cell.*

"You pushed me." Her voice went flat.

I didn't deny it.

After that, she ran off to the condo and secluded herself behind the bedroom's closed door.

I climbed up to the loft. I closed my eyes. I fell into the darkness and found sleep, oblivious of the cove's clamor. Mostly, it must have been the clatter of my own jangled thoughts.

Yet, a few hours later, I awoke, terrified. *How could I have almost killed her?*

No answers came to me. After several sleepless hours, my taxi arrived. Gloria didn't appear, and I never looked in to say good-bye.

### KEEPING QUIET

*A version of this story is part of my novel,* Making It Work. *While I was never accosted by someone like Leroy, like so many women I have been in vulnerable situations. Somehow I learned how to confront the people who invaded my space, but it wasn't an easy learning experience. Sheila, the protagonist in my novel, remembers a time when she was young, was in a risky spot, and used her voice. My Minnesota family used to gather in the summer for family picnics. I always found these to be fun times. The familiar setting seemed like a good place to start, as I imagined details of Sheila's fictional family.*

# Keeping Quiet

Published by *Limestone*, December 2015

One of the stories Lily told her daughter started like this: "On a Saturday summer night in 1946, Thor barged into my life." Lily was the youngest of the five children who never referred to him as their "father."

Lily and Carl Doty's cramped apartment was upstairs from his widowed mother's house in the little town of Chambers, Minnesota. Carl, home from serving in the Navy, worked at the flour mill and at weekends tended the bar at Bernie's, a few blocks away. On this night, even though her husband was gone, Lily felt nothing but peacefulness and pleasure rocking and nursing three-month-old Sheila, until she heard a clunk—clunk—clunk of heavy boots on the wooden steps that clung to the house's back wall. The bang—bang—bang of a fist on the door came next. She was sure that her mother-in-law, a heavy sleeper, had long since gone to bed downstairs. Lily almost didn't answer the door. Who could be stopping by after nine at night? But, Lily later told Sheila, "I couldn't hide like a frightened mouse. I was a wife and a mother. An adult."

After hearing this story so many times, Sheila, at ten or eleven, began to make up her own mental pictures of Lily buttoning a bodice with one hand, pushing fine blonde hair back, and tucking a pink blanket around her. Then, Lily answered the door.

Standing under the porch light, a brown felt hat pulled down so that it almost concealed his heavy-lidded, pale-blue eyes, a fist raised and ready to pound again, stood her father. "I hadn't seen him in years and stared at him, speechless," Lily would say.

"Been to Bernie's. Heard about my new granddaughter." Thor announced with his gruff-as-an-ogre's voice.

Sheila imagined Lily pulling her close so tight that she yowled.

"You never stopped screeching while he hulked at our door."

"Great lungs." Thor stared into Sheila's flushed, scrunched features.

"Several times I tried to cover your face with the blanket," Lily continued.

Tiny fists flailing, Sheila tossed the blanket aside.

"Your look seemed to declare, 'Do not touch!'"

"Aren't you going to invite your father in?" the ogre said.

Lily thrust out her pointed chin and, for the first time ever, stood up to Thor. "I have to put my baby to bed." With that, she slammed and bolted the door and collapsed against it. "A minute or so later, I heard his heavy boots descending the stairway."

A bit past two on Sunday morning, after the bar closed, Carl tiptoed up those same steps. He entered the apartment and found lights ablaze and his wife, wide awake and frightened.

"Why did you tell him I was here?"

"Never did!" Carl's brown eyes snapped, darkening to almost black. "If I find out who told, they'll answer to me." His fists clenched, ready to strike. "He came in. I ignored him. The boss would've let me come home early if we figured Thor was headed this way." Bernie Olsen, along with everyone else in Chambers, knew of Thorvald Norstad's meanness.

"It's all right," Lily said, relaxing now that Carl filled the apartment with his presence. "He won't come back. Sheila was in my arms and yelled as soon as I opened the door. She scared him off."

Carl gently held Lily. "Don't worry. I'll never let him hurt you again."

"Your father gazed into the bassinet at you." She would smile at Sheila. "His face, a moment before scary, returned to an easy smile, dimples deepening. He touched your cheek at your very own dimple, and said, 'None the worse for her ordeal.'"

"Little as she is, Sheila has good instincts," Lily told him.

"You've got a headache, don't you?" Carl lifted her chin. "Let's get you into bed."

Later, Sheila knew that he poured her a tumbler full of whiskey, too.

Lily would end her story with, "You sensed danger and wickedness the minute it came near."

This became her mother's myth: Sheila attracted good and repelled evil. Though sweet of face and disposition, Sheila possessed a powerful voice to go along with her fiery red hair.

Lily also said, "You're the strong one. Take care of your little brother." According to other stories of her mother's, Tommy, three years younger than Sheila, was weak like Lily and seemed to attract trouble wherever he went.

Having heard it over and over again, this became one of Sheila's stories.

\*\*\*

Each summer as she grew up, her mother's family never failed to gather for a picnic reunion in some Minnesota town to which the relations could easily drive. These get-togethers were always the same. Women toted covered bowls and platters of fried chicken, potato and macaroni salads with mayonnaise that soon curdled, fruit salad with runny whipped cream, and homemade pickles, as well as cherry and apple pies, chocolate and angel food cakes, peanut butter, oatmeal raisin, and sugar cookies. The married women, housewives all, tended to the set-up, serve-up, and clean-up—while catching up.

Sheila would watch her mother listening to the other women, especially her older sisters, Magda and Selma. These women gathered at a long stretch of picnic tables, carried over and lined up by the men. Lily sipped from a bottle of Hamms, ran her finger over a scratch on the table, and occasionally dropped in a remark about some ongoing health complaint—headaches, cramps, lack of energy—while the rest of the women concentrated on weddings, new babies, and funerals.

Since Sheila didn't want to play softball with the cousins, she was told by her mother to stay nearby. At the fringes of clustered adults, she huddled on a blanket with a book open in her lap.

Off to one side, the men would lounge beneath shady oak trees on lawn chairs, smoking, drinking beer, and talking livestock, crops, weather, and coming harvests. Only Carl Doty worked in the city, but he held up more than his share of the conversation with remarks about a demanding, always frustrating, job as an electrician where he answered to a "dumb shit" shop owner.

After the men and the women, still grouped separately, had stuffed themselves with too much food, and tongues had loosened from plenty of beer, without exception, a time of painful recollections came before packing up to leave. They'd nibble at crumbled cookies, and most of them would drink strong, black coffee. Now, the Norstad siblings compared hurts and shames and wicked deeds done to them by their father. These early evening ponderings closely resembled what might have been called "group therapy sessions" rather than end-of-the-day summings-up.

This telling ritual invariably started for the men when Carl said something like, "What do you think the Old Man did with his riches?"

The two Norstad brothers, Hans and Peter, would shake their heads, befuddled by the mystery of it all, and regretful because he sure hadn't given anything to them. Meanwhile, the other married-in men sat, not saying a thing, perhaps disgusted by the nature of Thor's misdeeds or bored by the repetition.

Thor had deserted his wife, Emma, and children in 1935, when Lily was only eight years old. Emma died a few years later, her illness caused, the siblings agreed, by difficulties maintaining a farm situated on dry, barren land. Magda and Selma finished bringing up Lily and cared for the house, while Hans and Peter managed the fields and livestock. Occasionally, the family received word from renters that their father, roaming the countryside, had sold some of his more productive land. Alliances with several women, apparently resulting in no half-siblings, were also reported. The last one to see Thor had been Lily in 1946.

With this part of their memories covered, the men slipped into talk of other paternal abuses—beatings, deprivation of food, lack of proper clothing.

Off to their side, still sitting at the picnic tables, the married-in women spoke loudly of their own troubles. Magda and Selma, in tones so quiet that Sheila barely heard and wished that she hadn't, spoke to Lily of terrible things Thor had done "to his own daughters."

Aunt Magda, glancing over toward her brothers, whispered to Aunt Selma, "At least...weren't violated...personal ways."

"...lucky ones..." Aunt Selma whispered back.

"...never the same..." Revulsion would twist Aunt Magda's ruddy features.

Aunt Selma returned to the handiwork in her lap. Scrutinizing it—pulling on a thread here, tying a knot there—speaking no further.

"Lily...favored one...spared," Aunt Magda seemed compelled to say, and louder, "He was long gone when you were still a child."

"I had some beatings," Lily always responded. "Mama died before I was grown."

"You were far from alone. You had us." Aunt Magda would sweep a hand to include Aunt Selma, and then softer, "What...trials compared to...loss..."

"Quiet now. What's past is past." Aunt Selma would reach her hand out to stroke Lily's shoulders that were scrunched up to her ears.

The picnics ended with important things said: offenses recounted, assurances repeated.

It was not their fault.

***

On this particular picnic, held at the Pine Falls City Park in 1960, when Sheila was thirteen, the weather was of primary concern. The humid air made clothes stick to their bodies. Black clouds threatened to open with a deluge. When they weren't looking toward the sky, the other big topic was politics because of the upcoming national election. They were all Democrats.

Uncle Hans said, "Do you think Kennedy can possibly win? Being a Catholic?"

"Here's hoping," Uncle Peter said, and everyone nodded.

"That shouldn't make any difference." Carl had grown up Catholic, yet stayed home while his converted wife and children headed off to Mass each Sunday.

Sitting on her blanket, Sheila turned from her book and assessed her father, noting how his dark features stood out against the Norstad blondness.

These others, all Lutherans, grew silent, eyes cast down, except for Aunt Magda, who said, "I don't care if Jack Kennedy is Catholic. What a fine-looking man."

"With such a beautiful wife and little girl." Aunt Selma pursed her lips. "She's expecting, you know."

Once the ominous weather that never changed, the presidential election, and the mundane had been fully discussed; once the food and beer had been consumed, the siblings got around to the same old thing—the cruelties of their father.

"What do you suppose he did with the return on your crops?" Carl began the litany.

"Put it toward another repossessed farm." Uncle Peter's white stripe of forehead wrinkled toward his receding hairline.

"Profited from that owner's bad luck," Uncle Hans's back slumped turtle-like.

"Those farmers got a share. More than Hans and me ever saw," Uncle Peter added.

"The hell you say." Leroy's words were hoarse from a constant wad of tobacco. He was Cousin Beverly's second husband and a newcomer. Sheila found him to be strange—the way he nudged Ronnie, Beverly's older child, and leered at the girls; the way he talked to Beverly's ten-year-old daughter, Laurie, criticizing her ruffly pastel shirts in a teasing way that still made the girl squirm.

Sheila wanted to holler at him to leave Laurie alone. Of course, she stifled her words.

And, there was the way Leroy listened so intently to the men's stories.

"It's every word God's own truth," Uncle Hans said. "Wily as an old wolf. By this time probably long-dead."

"Never missed." Uncle Peter sneered. "Father's are supposed to lead their families."

Thor had cheated his sons only once. He offered the young men, who were in their early twenties, parcels of land and a percentage of the profit for their labor. After harvest, he secretly pocketed every cent. From then on, Peter and Hans sought out dependable wages paid by honest local farmers.

Sheila had heard too many stories about her awful grandfather. She wasn't a little kid anymore. She decided to sneak off to her father's Chevy, parked across the baseball field, where she could finish her book—Gone with the Wind—undisturbed. Edging away from the adults, she saw that no one looked at her anyhow. Waving cigarettes, spilling coffee, or in the case of her mother, beer, fussing with handiwork, they'd never miss her.

She hunched down in the car's backseat and, as dusk gathered, read those last few pages. With Scarlett's words, "Tomorrow's another day," Sheila held the book close and wept. Gradually, her misty-gray eyes closed and she dozed off, never putting it down.

"Wha'cha doin' out here all by yourself?"

Leroy's gravelly voice awakened Sheila with a jolt. She kept her eyes tightly shut, thinking, he must be headed to the outhouse. If I stay quiet, he'll go away.

Leroy eased open the car door and slid in next to her. "Why d'ya want to be holed up reading?"

She'd heard him ask questions like this of other girl cousins: "How come you wear that orange lipstick?" or "Is that all you do—play softball?" or, to his stepdaughter, Laurie, "Don't you want to help your mother with the food? Make the men happy?" These girls—there were four in addition to Sheila—turned fidgety, stammering confused replies.

"Because this is where I want to be."

"Snippy—snippy." Leroy's lip jerked up.

"You can't make me feel bad." Sheila clenched her jaw.

"Why would I want to do that?" Leroy took Sheila's book, fingers trailing across the front of her yellow halter top. He moved in close enough so that she could smell his spicy aftershave and a sharp, acrid odor underneath. "What's special about this?" His words were tinged with amusement. "Gone Wi—"

Sheila grabbed for it as Leroy held the book high and rested his other hand on the back of her neck. "You want?" That hand squeezed hard enough to make a sharp pain shoot to her head. "Be nice."

She stretched to a taller sitting position, and Leroy's hand slid down, resting on the bow at her mid-back. She gave him a shove and frantically peered toward the faraway adults. Talking and talking and talking. Please see me trapped. No one looked her way. Scarlett came to mind. Sheila said, "Get away from me!" She jabbed Leroy with her elbow.

"You're a tiger." He grasped her wrist. "Real uppity."

"If you don't leave this car this minute, I'll scream so loud they'll all come running." Would anyone hear?

"I just wanted to look at your storybook."

"Go away!" Sheila let out a wail. And, like she had done as an infant, never stopped hollering until Leroy jumped from the car.

"All right. I'm gone." He threw the book at Sheila, grazing her cheek with its hard corner. Slamming the door, he said, "You can't fool me. You wanted attention. You're a little tease." He spat a long stream of brown onto the ground.

"You're dead wrong."

Sheila waited, rubbing her face, watching his retreating back. After he slipped like a weasel back into the group, she began to consider, Did I say something to him? Did I look at him in some way? Sheila couldn't think of a thing she had done.

A few minutes later she ran across the grass to where Lily sat.

Her mother casually put a thin, bare arm around Sheila's waist. "Almost time to go," she said, oblivious to the girl's breathlessness. Lily's white, sleeveless shirt and navy-blue pedal pushers, that she had taken so much time pressing earlier in the day, were rumpled and stained from serving and cleaning. "Have a good time?" She tipped a bottle to her lips.

Sheila considered what to say. I can't upset her. A sickness would follow. She pictured her father's fury and could hear his words—He'll have hell to pay! It would ruin the picnic for everyone. "I had fun."

"What happened to your face?"

"Scratched on a branch."

"Be more careful. You don't want to scar." Lily stifled a hiccup and turned, with a defensive expression, back to the conversation.

Aunt Magda was telling about how their mother pampered and indulged Lily. "She knew how to get her own way."

\*\*\*

The storm held off until their dark drive home. Sheila pressed against a corner of the backseat, behind her mother. In the flashes of lightning she watched ten-year-old Tommy, head against his window, feigning sleep. Her father hadn't caught him smoking behind the pavilion.

Sheila had seen him, and warned, "Dad's gonna give you one heck of a beating if he finds out."

"How will that happen? You won't tell."

She never would.

After the picnics, Carl talked about his wife's family and their ordeals for a good long while. The monologues always ended when Lily said, "I sure was lucky that you came along to save me." Carl would push his spread hands into the wheel, steering with his large palms.

On this drive home in 1960, after he had hashed over the same territory and Lily reiterated her good fortune, after another crack of thunder, Carl turned to a new subject. Sensing the change, Sheila quit worrying about Tommy as well as Scarlett's future, and tuned in on her parents.

"I don't know what it is about Ronnie. He reminds me of the Old Man."

Ronnie wasn't that much ahead of Sheila—fifteen maybe. She found him to be boring with his round, bland face and heavy-lidded, pale-blue eyes.

"Why would you say that?" Lily's voice tightened.

"His look." Carl took a drag from a Lucky Strike. "That waiting-to-take-advantage look."

"I don't see it."

"It's there," he persisted. "I know Ronnie's had it hard. Good thing Leroy came along. To father the boy. Beverly's damned fortunate she found someone to marry her with two kids in the bargain."

Sheila recalled those nudges Leroy gave Ronnie when a girl walked by, his head swaying with the movement of her hips. And, the way Laurie turned red when she got the least bit close to him.

"You can see how much he cares for Laurie. Complimenting her in that backhand way of his." Carl took another drag. "Mark my words, Ronnie should be watched."

"You're right," Lily agreed the way she always did. "So, you had a good time?"

"I enjoy being with your family. You know that." Avoiding a deep accumulation of rain, Carl swerved to the middle of the road, then quickly straightened the wheel.

Sheila wondered if Ronnie was really like her evil grandfather. Is that how he looked? Ronnie was a tall, heavyset kid—bigger than the other boys, but he never fought with them. He stared at the girls, but he never did anything—anything that she knew about. Not like his stepfather, Leroy. Sheila shivered, recalling his slithering hands. How could Cousin Beverly stand him? Did she know he acted like this? What about Laurie? Who should I tell? Can I tell anyone?

Her mother was happy. The storm had held off and the picnic had been another success. There'd be no headaches this night. Her father was happy. In his usual way, he'd sparked up the Norstads. Sheila didn't know if Tommy was happy or not. Soon, she'd be home to her own dry bedroom, all her books, where she could forget about this day. It would be a whole year until another family picnic.

# BELONGING

I went to a camp similar to the one described in my story, "Belonging," and I had a very good friend for several years who went to the same camp. At some point, around sixth grade, she rejected me. Who hasn't experienced the pain of rejection by someone you cared about a lot? The characters and the circumstances in the story are all fictional; however, this one-time-friend was actually chosen "Best All-Around Camper" at the end of the session when she rejected me. This made me feel even more unworthy. I couldn't figure out why everyone else thought she was so wonderful. But, as with most hurts like this, I went on, had many other close friends, and for the most part forgot about this old friend and the hurt she caused me. However, not completely, because she was the inspiration for this story.

# *Belonging*

Published by *Goldman Review*, November 2016

It was our first time at St. Barnabas Episcopal Church. We huddled in a back pew, my head resting on Mom's arm, Markie fidgeting on her other side.

Reverend Newton stood in front of the altar and announced in a booming voice that made me jerk upright: "The Youth Choir starts today. Besides joy in praising God with song, each member will earn two weeks at Camp Duncan. So, children, see you in the loft." He pointed at three pews to the side.

Gathering her purse and sweater for a quick exit, Mom said, "Do you want to join the choir, Anne?"

I can see myself, with pleading, brown eyes, saying, "I really do."

"Your father will have to wait to eat." She cooked delicious Sunday dinners of fried chicken or pot roast. Turning to my little brother, she went on, "If Anne's doing this, you can sing in the choir too."

"I want to stay," Markie whined.

"It might be fun."

With a sniff of disgust, I grabbed his hand.

We had moved to another Minneapolis apartment, the fifth in my seven years. Dad kept promising that someday we'd have a real house. When he found employment as a bricklayer, he brought in good money. When he didn't have a job, which happened through the winter months, at least there wasn't much rent. He and Mom were caretakers in these many buildings, each a better deal than the last. This Hopper Street apartment, in a gloomy basement, looked out on an alley. The raucous shouts of garbage collectors and the *bang—bang—bang* of barrels being emptied awakened me every Tuesday morning.

It took several minutes for the choir director, Mrs. Ashworth, who had a huge bosom pooching out from a low, round neckline, to organize the twenty or so children gathered. A subdued Markie hovered close to me. The other boys tussled like a pack of friendly mutts. The girls chattered like a farmyard full of hens. One girl, with inky-dark blue eyes and a face blank as an empty page, stood against the wall, watching. She had been in my Sunday School class. Tilting her head toward me, she squinted as if measuring my height.

Eventually we were arranged in the loft. I was placed in the front pew and Markie at the end of the back pew. He looked ready to bolt. To my right, closest to the altar, sat Emily Price, the watchful girl. She was half a head taller than me.

Mrs. Ashworth took a deep breath, her bosom rising like a bowl of bread dough, and clapped her hands to quiet the ruckus. "I want to teach you one of my favorites—'The Saints of God.'"

This hymn brought pictures to my mind: folks at tea; a shepherdess on the green; a knight killing some fierce, wild beast.

"In a month I want you to sing for the congregation," Mrs. Ashworth said. "Do you think we can make that happen?"

No one responded.

"Remember, participation in choir means two weeks at Camp Duncan."

"Yessss, Mrs. Ashworth," we said in unison.

*"I sing a song of the saints of God/Patient and brave and true…"*

In half an hour Mrs. Ashworth said, "That's enough for today."

Emily shifted toward me. "You have a really good voice."

"So do you." It seemed polite to say this, even though, while floating off to faraway places with my singing, I hadn't noticed.

"Let's get some cookies."

"Sure, but I have to bring my brother." He was nowhere to be seen.

Upon entering the church hall, I spotted Mom. Markie stood behind her like a shadow. She sipped coffee, listening to a woman who kept waving a hand back and forth as if leading the choir herself. This woman's black hair streaked with gray made her look like someone's grandma.

"That's my mother," Emily said.

Mrs. Price wasn't partnered up with a man. I soon found out that Emily's father, similar to my own, never went to church.

"Can Anne come to play?" she asked.

"Certainly," Mrs. Price said. "How about this afternoon?"

"Do you want to?" Mom leaned close and I caught a whiff of something fresh, like the fragrance of early morning flowers.

"I do." Visiting other people's real houses, with plenty of room for everyone, fascinated me.

I hopped in the backseat of Mrs. Price's blue Oldsmobile next to Emily and gave a cheerful wave to Mom and Markie, standing hand-in-hand on the curb. At the time I failed to see how deserted they must have looked. A pine-smelling cardboard tree hung from the car's rearview mirror. It failed to cover up the odor of cigarettes.

***

St. Barnabas, with its grand history, stood down the block from our building. The mayor and university president attended. Many of the families lived in mansions on Lake Beckwith Boulevard, a few miles from the Hopper Street neighborhood. In between was Emily's three-story, stucco house on Oldhaven Avenue.

Standing on the sidewalk, I thought, *It's big!* I didn't notice the peeling blue trim.

Inside Emily pointed to a pink powder room. "Let's wash up." In our apartment there was one all-purpose bathroom with a tub/shower.

On the way to dinner, I peeked at the living room. Hundreds of books filled built-in shelves.

Once we were seated at the shiny mahogany table, I waited for someone to say Grace. Mom and Markie and I prayed before meals. Instead Mr. Price said, "Pass your plates," with that same blank face Emily often assumed. He carved the chicken, which looked as dark as a Brazil nut.

She and I asked for white meat.

"They want breasts." Her oldest brother, Geoffrey, was about sixteen.

Pretending not to hear him, I spread a thick, paper napkin across my lap. Each of the others had silver rings with white, linen napkins rolled inside. Loopy, engraved letters made the rings look like something for royalty. I later realized these were called monograms and that the silver needed polishing.

Once everyone started to eat, I pressed my fork into lumpy mashed potatoes and stirred mushy mixed vegetables. A fancy chandelier made up for what the meal lacked. At that time I didn't see cobwebs winding through the candle-like lights. My food tasted as bland as dry toast. Still, I ate everything.

Mrs. Price said, "Do you want another serving?"

"Yes, please."

She smiled broadly, showing yellow teeth.

"As much as you eat, you should be bigger than Em." Geoffrey leered at me.

I scrunched lower in my chair.

"Rude!" The other brother, Bradley, was about a year younger than Geoffrey.

The two boys went to St. Barnabas High, where Emily attended elementary school.

Mrs. Price, who, according to Emily, spent all her time doing "guild stuff," talked during that first dinner about new altar cloths and people who dedicated floral arrangements and an upcoming wedding of a Lake Beckwith neighborhood couple.

Mr. Price wore a blue sweater draped over his shoulders. He didn't say a word after serving our chicken. By contrast, my talkative father brought up the Democratic Party and upcoming elections and unions while we ate.

I learned that Mr. Price sailed in the summer and skied in the winter and worked in Mrs. Price's father's stock brokerage and seldom read a thing. When we were by ourselves, Emily filled me in on lots of family details.

Near the meal's conclusion Mrs. Price said, "You didn't clean your plate, Emily. No dessert."

Pushing the last of some peas onto a fork with my pointer, I waited for anything tasty.

"Anne dear, use a bit of dinner roll, not your fingers," Mrs. Price said.

I hid my hands in my lap.

(After Mrs. Price dropped me off at the apartment, I filled my mother in on the wonders of Emily's house and some of my awkward moments. When I told her about rolls for pushers, she blurted out, "Well...I never!")

While Mrs. Price stepped away for dessert, Emily said, "I'll wait 'til you finish the bananas and cottage cheeeese."

Not even a cherry. My mother would have put this yucky stuff out as an optional side dish. I took a tiny bite and said, "I'm sorry. I'm full."

Geoffrey said, "It's about time."

Bradley said, "Nasty!"

"That's enough, boys," Mrs. Price said. "You girls may be excused."

***

A large room took up almost the whole third floor. Streaky dormer windows faced the street. There were three doors, one to a bathroom. Used towels strewn around made a musty smell, like in a swimming pool's changing area. The other closed doors went to Geoffrey's and Bradley's bedrooms. A slouchy, gray sofa sat across from the television. I figured Mr. and Mrs. Price came up here for programs.

My parents snuggled every night on our tan sofa for Milton Berle, *The Honeymooners*, or *I Love Lucy*. In hysterics, Markie and I would roll around on the linoleum when the ditzy lady pulled her antics.

A metal climbing structure, like a jungle gym at the park across two busy streets from our building, filled one corner. A wooden slide, about which Emily said, "Be careful. You might get a sliver," stood beside it. A trapeze was bolted into the high ceiling. "Look what I can do!" She hung from her knees. Her dress made a tent around her face, revealing tattered, white underpants. A dollhouse, tucked in a dormer, looked like one of the brick mansions on Lake Beckwith Boulevard. She said, "My grandfather built that for me. It's an exact replica of where Mother grew up."

"Did your father live by her?"

"He came from inner-city Chicago."

I wasn't sure what "inner-city" meant but decided that the Hopper Street neighborhood, with its once-beautiful buildings, might be described this way.

***

The next Saturday Markie said, "I'll go to Sunday School, but I'm not singing in that dumb choir."

"What about you, Anne?"

"I want to do it all. Will I be invited over to Emily's?"

"I don't know but you need to reciprocate."

"What's that mean?"

"She should visit here."

"Alright." I looked into Markie's and my bedroom, cluttered with Tinker Toys and Lincoln Logs and trucks, hoping her visit wouldn't happen for a long time.

Mom got a call from Mrs. Price that very day. Afterward I heard her say to Dad, "...awfully bossy..." and "...almost demanded..."

I got to go for a sleepover.

In her second floor room, Emily gestured to a twin bed. "That's yours."

Her carpet, where we sat cross-legged and played Go to the Dump, was dark green and velvety-feeling except on the worn spots. The wallpaper that came apart at a few seams was covered with lilacs, making it feel as if we were sitting on the ground with high, blooming bushes all around. Next to the bedroom was her very own bathroom with a claw-footed tub.

Across a hall, wide as the one by my principal's office, was another large room with a single bed.

"That's where Mother sleeps," Emily said.

As I studied the room, she added, "My father sleeps in his den downstairs."

On weekend mornings Markie and I crowded in our parents' bed. The sheets carried a sweet smell like my mother.

That night Emily and I ate toasted cheese sandwiches and watched television in the third floor room that we had to ourselves because the boys were out.

"When will your mom and dad come up here?"

"He's always gone on Saturday night—all night." Emily shrugged.

When we got tired, she led me back down to the second floor. I saw Mrs. Price in her bedroom, sitting on a green brocade-covered chair, listening to what, in the future, I identified as Bach. She never looked up from stitching needlepoint. A crystal tumbler of brown liquid sat on a small table next to her. Beside the tumbler a matching crystal ashtray held her smoldering cigarette.

"Bradley says Mother's booze helps her sleep," Emily said.

\*\*\*

She became my weekend best friend—a lucky thing because our family continued to move, causing me to change regular schools and every-other-day best friends almost annually. Music had brought us together, and we continued to sing much of the time. Her favorite pop song was "Blue Suede Shoes." Emily wiggled her hips and did an imitation of Elvis, dark hair slicked back with her father's Brylcreem. "You can be Pat Boone," she would say. "Your soft hair is the same color as his." My song was "April Love."

Occasionally Emily did stay with us. I shoved all Markie's junk in the closet beforehand, and he slept on the sofa.

One Saturday night we piled into Dad's old Ford and went to a drive-in movie. *Raintree County* was playing.

"That was great," Emily said afterward, and I agreed, even though parts had gone over my head.

Before the next day's church service, I heard Mrs. Price telling Mom, "That was not an appropriate film for the girls."

My mother rolled her eyes. Markie and I followed her into a back pew while Mrs. Price and Emily headed for theirs up front.

\*\*\*

In the summer we took a bus to Camp Duncan on Woods Lake— a session for girls up to sixth grade. Seven of us and a teenaged counselor stayed in each cabin. Almost always, Emily and I shared a bunkbed with her on top. At campfire singalongs we started out with songs like "John Jacob Jingleheimer Schmidt," rocking our bodies back and forth. Everyone agreed I should do solos. Singing something like "The Saints of God," I'd tingle from my toes on up to my ponytail. We'd end chanting the "Nunc dimittis" while gazing into glimmering embers, our shirts and shorts and hair picking up the smell of smoke, our shoulders touching.

*"Lord, now lettest thou thy servant depart in peace..."*

The last night of camp we had a special program. Each cabin performed a skit and awards were presented. I usually received Best Singer and Emily received Best Swimmer. A special honor was Best All Around Camper, given to a sixth grader.

The first four years are a happy blur. I remember crying each time our session was over, and Emily, close to me on a bus seat, saying, "I wish we could live together forever."

The fifth year remains etched in my mind.

***

After our idyllic fourth time, Emily became too busy to talk on the telephone or get together. She and Bradley were crewing on her father's sailboat.

At last autumn arrived and she invited me for a Saturday overnight.

Sixth grade was still elementary school for me, but Emily's sixth grade was the start of junior high. Her brother Geoffrey attended the University of Minnesota, where he lived in a fraternity house. Bradley didn't go to college or work and still lived at home.

In the afternoon Emily took me to Geoffrey's old room and reached under the mattress and pulled out a worn magazine. "This is *Playboy*...what do you think?"

A blonde woman spread across the middle pages had a bare bosom, as big as Mrs. Ashworth's, but the rest of her was much smaller. "Didn't she get embarrassed?"

Emily scrutinized me in her blank way before pushing that magazine back under the mattress.

We were in her bathroom, bobby-pinning our hair into elaborate styles that fell out as soon as we moved, when she said, "I'll bet your parents have sex all the time."

I held my comb mid-air. "I don't know."

"They're always hugging."

Mom had told me about sex and said it was special, for when you were married. I thought they'd done it twice because this was the way to get Markie and me.

Emily glanced sideways. "Dad does it with Roberta." And, with my questioning expression, "She's the receptionist at The Club."

"How do you know?"

"Bradley told me she's his mistress."

It was a stifling evening, and we sat on Emily's porch swing until the sun went down, singing some of our old favorites, swaying rhythmically: "Mairzy Doats" and "White Coral Bells" and "Frere Jacques."

Suddenly she dragged her foot, causing the swing to lurch to a stop. "I know what to do with my boyfriend when the time comes...Bradley showed me." Her shoulders squared for a few seconds before they crumpled. Then she started swinging faster than ever and we quit singing.

After our toasted cheese sandwiches upstairs, we settled into the familiar twin beds in her garden-like room. Once the lights were off, she said, "I have a boyfriend."

"You do?"

"We've kissed lots of times. I let him feel me up."

I bunched the blanket around my ears and pretended to fall asleep.

\*\*\*

Emily's new choir friend, Monica, lived in the Lake Beckwith neighborhood, went to St. Barnabas School, and had a boyfriend too. When I heard that she and this girl would be bunkmates at camp the following summer, a gripping pain settled in under my tiny developing breasts. *I'm not going!*

Mrs. Ashworth said, "This'll be your last year. They need your lovely voice."

I ignored her.

My mother said, "It would be a chance to practice your singing."
So I changed my mind.

The other girls at camp were paired up, except for me and fat, pimply Frances, who lived by Monica. We were assigned to be bunkmates in a cabin several doors away from Emily's. Everywhere I went Frances tagged along, jabbering, "It's so much fun doing things together."

From afar I watched Emily and Monica, whispering and laughing and giving each other easy pokes. One afternoon they were missing for hours. Counselors flew into a tizzy until the two showed up for dinner, where they behaved as if nothing had happened.

Frances, who knew everything, said, "Their boyfriends hitchhiked out here and met them in the woods."

A day or so later, trying unsuccessfully to lose her, I headed down a deserted path to the boathouse. There huddled Emily and Monica, smoking.

Frances gave me a nudge. "Should we report them?"

"I don't want to be a tattletale."

Toward the end of our two weeks, Emily approached me. "Come to our cabin after lights out."

"Sure." I hoped she didn't see my trembling.

"Bring Frances if you can't get rid of her."

In the dark she and I entered Emily's cabin. Scantily dressed girls carried gleaming flashlights and talked in a garbled way and passed a bottle around.

The counselor, Monica's older sister, Sharon, said, "If you two want to belong in our club, you have to take your shirts off. Show us what you got."

Frances fumbled with a button as I backed away. "You don't have to do this." They would howl at the rolls of fat beneath her large breasts.

"I want to be part of their club."

"I'm leaving. You can go with me."

She shook her head.

Emily scowled at me. "You don't belong here anyhow."

I stumbled out the door and back to my cabin. I scrambled up to my bunk. I listened to the other girls' sighs and snores, trying to fall asleep on my wet pillow. When Frances crawled in the bottom bunk, I smelled something sort of sickly sweet and sort of like she'd thrown up. I heard muffled sobs which made me consider, *What's it like to be a Lake Beckwith neighborhood girl who'll never fit in?*

We had our special program the last night. All I wanted was to go home. Still, I barely could conceal my disappointment when Reverend Newton handed out awards. A fourth grader who lived close to Frances and always went flat got Best Singer. Monica was chosen Friendliest. At last he dramatically cleared his throat and boomed, "I'm proud to announce Best All Around Camper for 1959. This year's choice goes to a girl we all love and respect—Emily Price."

***

In September Mom answered a telephone call and, after a minute, said, "I'm sorry, Mrs. Ashworth. Anne can't be in Advanced Choir. We've moved too far away. It won't be convenient to attend St. Barnabas any longer."

She hung up and saw me, and her face turned so red that the freckles disappeared. "You shouldn't have heard."

Truth was my parents were restoring an old brick house in the Hopper Street neighborhood with plenty of rooms for all of us.

"Singing in my junior high choir is better."

The next Sunday morning, while she stirred waffle batter in our torn-apart kitchen, I overheard Mom say to Dad, "I'll never have to put up with that woman again."

For a while I wanted to see Emily. For a while I wished she'd call so I could hang up. After a while I forgot about her—most of the time.

# DENIAL

*This story provided background information for a minor character in my novel,* Making It Work. *For the most part "Denial" is fictional, yet, years ago I was acquainted with a couple who came to mind when creating Eleanor and Nick. I barely knew this real couple, but was familiar with several of their close friends. Some of these friends were gossipy and there was an implication that the man in the couple had married the woman for her money and family status. I have no idea if this was the case, and I have had no contact with any of these people for decades, but when thinking about the character of Eleanor this barely-known couple simmered up through my subconscious. This is an example of the unusual nature of writing fiction. I never know why certain elements fall into place. This, for me, is one of the many magical elements.*

# Denial

Published by *Adelaide Magazine*, 2017

The yellow 1964 MGB my father gave me as a birthday present had been parked in front of our special place—Rose Motel—for three hours. We'd been meeting there for the past six months.

In Room 5, Nick and I sprawled across a lumpy, double bed, still naked and damp from lovemaking. One of my long, sticklike legs draped across his lower torso. My head nestled against his shoulder. I traced a hand along his stomach. Was it less fleshy? Was Nick, at seventeen, losing his pudginess? Just the year before we had been the same height of five-foot-ten. Lately, he'd been looking down at me instead of meeting eye to eye. My lips pursed into a smirk at the image of him towering over everyone in my family. The whole lot of them— Mother, my older brother Chet, my younger sister Marj, even my father—with their healthy, golden skin and compact, shorter-than-average bodies.

Picturing those sturdy, tanned people, I couldn't help but recall endless hours on Sunny Daze, the sailboat inherited from my maternal grandfather, Frederick Porterfield. The others would companionably holler back and forth above board while I hid below deck, playing my violin, going over and over difficult passages in pieces like Vivaldi's "La Tempesta di Mare."

Every half hour or so, Mother would yell down, "El - e - a - nor! Enough already!"

I had been named after my paternal grandmother—a name I'm sure Mother disliked but agreed to as a concession to my father. She'd parody it when annoyed with me, which was most of the time.

I'd take a break from my practice, feeling like a collapsed sail. Once I figured she was occupied with rigging, or whatever else happened up there, I resumed my music.

Now, moving away from Nick's warm body, I whispered, "We have to talk."

"Huh?" He roused from a doze.

"Please wake up. I need to tell you something." I placed a pillow behind my back and drew the sheet over my breasts, self-conscious even though he called them his "beautiful little lemons."

One of his brown eyes squinted open as he rasped, "What's up?"

"My acceptance from Middlebury came yesterday. I'm going to Vermont."

It was December of our senior years—mine at Oak Ridge, a private girls' school on the fringes of Porterfield, Connecticut; his at Roosevelt, a public high school in the warehouse district. August seemed an eternity away, yet I knew we had to think about this if my plan were to work, if Nick were to go with me. I had purposefully chosen Middlebury over Mother's Wellesley because it was co-ed.

"I want you to apply."

Nick sat up and I caught a whiff of his English Leather. He stuffed a pillow behind his back. "Even if I could get in, how do I pay? No one's going to give me a scholarship."

"I have a plan."

"Yeah?"

"Let's get married." We had never used protection, and I had secretly wished for a pregnancy to force the issue. But, no such luck. "Right after graduation."

"Your mother won't allow it."

"We'll elope."

"What's that got to do with you going to Vermont?" His dark eyebrows scrunched together.

"She'd never, ever, want me to skip college, and you can go too. My father will pay."

"Your father?"

"Of course."

Daddy didn't have much to do with Nick, who showed no interest in Sunny Daze or playing tennis, but unlike Mother, he'd never been nasty. She made remarks like, "He's not our kind, dear." Daddy said things like, "If he makes you happy, he's all right with me." My father knew what it was like to be poor. He'd been a scholarship student when he met my mother. And, after that he did whatever it took to keep things agreeable for her. If it meant paying for my new husband's education, as well as my own, Daddy, who ran Porterfield Textiles since my grandfather's death, would go for it.

Taking in Nick's puzzled expression, I said, "Trust me. This'll all work out."

***

Walking around campus with my handsome husband, I felt as if I possessed some enviable treasure—like a trunk full of gold coins and jewels. Other girls stared at him, which gave me a secret smile. He was mine. Rushing to keep up with him, I could tell by his lengthened stride that their attention also pleased him. By the end of freshman year, he had reached six-foot-four, his chest broadened, his waist slimmed, and his ruddy skin, though scarred from adolescent acne, had a masculine, outdoor look, as if he spent all his spare time in the wind and spray. He'd also gotten rid of the glasses, opting for contact lenses. Along with physical changes, something else had occurred. His grandmother, whom he'd lived with since his unwed mother was killed in a car accident when he was three, died shortly after we married. Nick was adrift except for me.

I didn't delude myself. I still looked the same—tall, with scant curves, hunched shoulders, and a plain face that, while not unpleasant, resembled the cautious demeanor of a church cleaning lady. Despite this, with distance from the family, my self-confidence blossomed in direct proportion to the clearing of eczema that had plagued me since childhood.

At thirteen, Nick and I had met in a dermatologist's office. The state paid for him to make a few visits.

While he paged through a car magazine, I sat across from him, in an otherwise empty waiting room. Thoughtfully rubbing my hand on the pebbly upholstery of a chair, I decided that this boy, with his blotchy face, seemed nonthreatening. Bolstering my courage, I moved over beside him. He didn't look up. After a minute or two, I said, "That red car's a Corvette, right?" My question started a friendship, and a couple of years later, it became our romance.

\*\*\*

One day, the end of junior year, we took our last exam and headed across campus. I anticipated a long summer with plenty of time to play my violin, read anything I wanted to read, and explore fun places together.

"Let's sit down." Nick tossed his books on a stone bench.

"Aren't you ready for lunch?"

"I want to talk first. Here. Not at the apartment."

I sat next to him and put a hand on his knee. "Are you upset about something?"

"Not at all." He moved his leg. "I'm excited. I just don't want you to be upset."

"Why would I be upset?" I made a move to stroke his rough cheek, but he drew away and started scratching at a gouge in the bench.

"I'm not going back to school next fall."

His words sank in. "What do you mean? What will you do?"

"I'm not cut out for this stuff, El. You love it. I don't. I don't care that Michelangelo spent four years on his back painting that ceiling." He looked me full in the face. "The past few weeks have felt like four years to me."

I clutched my arms as if to protect myself from a storm at sea.

"I've been talking to Mike."

I grew uneasy when Nick talked to this Mike guy during class breaks. He was swarthy, with grease under his fingernails, not someone I wanted to be around. Meanwhile, I made an effort to talk to some of the girls, while trying to disguise how much I watched Nick out of the corner of my eye. The situation made me feel like a hovering, overprotective mother, but I couldn't help myself.

"His dad owns a garage. The old guy's sick and forced to retire. Mike's quitting school to take over. He wants me to work with him." Nick assessed my reaction, then sat up straighter. "I start tomorrow."

"No asking my opinion? What am I supposed to do while you're working all summer?" Suddenly, I felt rudderless, and my usually controlled voice had escalated to a shriek. A group of girls strolling by stopped and turned, like a flock of ducks on a pond. They gave Nick a quick once-over, then paddled away. This time their attention didn't make me feel the least bit pleased.

"I knew you'd be upset, and I'm really sorry, but I can't back down." He put an arm around my "bony frame," which he'd taken to teasing me about—in a loving way. "Let's go home. There's the rest of today. We can make the most of it."

I peered at him, almost able to touch the waves of enthusiasm emanating from his body. More than anything, I wanted him to be happy.

"Okay." I rose from the bench, already resigned to the future. The beginnings of a familiar tingle made me quicken my step.

That's how it worked—easily distracted. Whenever I grew bothered by something Nick did or didn't do, even though I seldom said anything, he sensed it, and at the earliest possible moment we were in our bedroom, where he stroked and plucked my body like a well-tuned instrument, his hands working me into a trembling, taut tension, until release was near, like the highest note on my violin, the piercing, exquisite sensation of a thin golden string running up through my insides, stretching tighter and tighter, until it could go no further...a sostenuto...followed by my soft exclamation and a tumbling down - down - down in a series of deepening tones.

***

I dropped by the garage every day, bringing lunch from a nearby deli. Nick seemed to appreciate each sandwich surprise. Often he would be with a customer, so I'd slip off to a corner of the grimy-smelling room, holding a brown bag and a Dr. Pepper, trying to be inconspicuous.

He'd be bent over an open hood, carefully tuning, adjusting, and pointing out different aspects of the engine, justifying services to be performed and explaining how the owner's car soon would be humming along in perfect order.

That fall, to my surprise, I enjoyed college on my own. I took appealing classes without worrying whether there would be anything remotely interesting for him. I played my violin with the campus orchestra. I attended marches against the war in Vietnam, and sometimes said to Nick, who had a medical deferment due to a heart murmur, "The U.S. government is lying to us. This is futile and senseless."

If happening to hear me, he'd mumble a vague response, then go back to his car magazine.

One day, I walked into the garage, and a girl from several of our classes the previous year stood next to him, looking into the engine of a purple Capri. Nick was in the midst of explaining the operations of her vehicle and his proposed alterations—as slowly and precisely as he did with any customer. At one point, he showed her how to test the car's oil level. After she (I remembered her name to be Heidi) pulled the dipstick out, wiped it off, reinserted it, pulled it back out, and showed Nick her results, I stepped forward with my deli offering.

"I didn't know you were here," Heidi said in a voice that sounded as languid as if she'd been awakened from a nap.

"I brought Nick's lunch." Why had I bothered to say this?

"That's right. You two are married. No wonder you watched this guy like such a hawk." She tossed her long, sun-streaked hair and laughed as if she'd said the funniest thing anyone had heard all day. Golden skin shone with her smile.

When Nick got home that night, early for a change, I mentioned Heidi. He shrugged it off.

A couple of hours later, he was extra attentive.

***

That spring, I was about to graduate. One day I stayed home alone making a special dinner for the two of us—to celebrate. Soon, my family would arrive for their blessedly brief visit. A knock startled me. Since no one ever dropped by, I assumed it to be the landlord returning our deposit. We'd given notice and planned a move to Washington,

D.C., where I would begin working at the Smithsonian in the department that planned multicultural presentations.

Putting on my pleasant face, I opened the door and found a middle-aged woman standing outside the apartment. Head bent down, she fingered buttons on her tan coat. A kerchief half covered her crimped, gray-brown curls.

"Yes?"

"You're Mrs. Duffek?" The woman raised her eyes for a moment, before casting them back to her buttons. One hung by a thread.

"I am. What is it?"

"My daughter…Heidi…she goes to the college."

"Maybe I know her."

"You do know her. She told me that she knows you and your husband."

"My husband?"

"That's why I'm here." The woman stared straight at me and took on a harsh attitude. "I want your husband to stay away from my Heidi. She shouldn't spend time with him. She's got a boyfriend to marry as soon as she's done with this college stuff. If he breaks it off, Heidi's going to be sorry. I don't want my girl hurt."

"You're mistaken. My husband works all day, and every night he's home with me." I pushed his occasional late hours from my mind. "You're thinking of someone else."

"I saw them together, Missus. Going into her apartment. My son…he's a patrolman…he checked the license I gave him. The car they came in belonged to your husband."

"Nick would never do anything like what you're implying. You need to leave and never come back!" I slammed the door and locked it.

Breathlessly, I collapsed onto the sofa, my cheeks burning. Hands rubbing my face, I spoke to the empty room. "There's an explanation. He repaired that purple Capri and he drove her…she had someone…the boyfriend…at her apartment. She needed to get money from him for the bill."

A couple of hours later, I heard the key turn. I'd been scrambling for what, if anything, to say. But while I waited, my skin had calmed. I was wearing my prettiest blue dress, the one that he said made my eyes look as clear as a cloudless June sky. "Yesterday"—one of his Beatles' records—played. I didn't care for most of his music, but did appreciate this group. Their instrumentals were good. Sometimes, like in this piece, there were violins playing.

"How come the door was locked? I told you I'd be home early."

"Um…I must have done it automatically…after Mr. Connor came by with our deposit."

Nick sniffed the air. "Something smells great." He always took my word on money matters. He pulled me to him and danced me around the room. He whispered, "What's the occasion?"

"We're leaving soon. I wanted to have a good-bye dinner to remember all the sweet times." I pressed my head into his chest. "I'm going to miss this place."

"Me too." He twirled me as the song ended, and said, "Anything happen today?"

I chose not to mention that crazy woman who'd been at our door. Why upset him over something as stupid as her accusations? Why spoil our meal? We had so much to be excited about. College was done. We were headed to Washington. I had a wonderful job. We'd signed papers on a house that my father bought for us in Alexandria, a short commute to the District. And, Daddy had helped Nick buy his own car repair shop, a couple of minutes from our new house. We were set. No. I won't say anything, I promised myself. What a strange woman. Spying on her daughter like that—not trusting her.

Nick put on another 45 and said, "Dinner can wait. Let's go this way." He started to sing with his deep voice, "Something in the way she moves…" He put his hand on the small of my back, guiding me into our bedroom. The whole day, along with the pot roast in the oven, disappeared from my mind as my skin began to glow, and I leaned into his gentle touch.

## CARNIVAL OF COLORS

*Several years ago I visited the small town in Western Minnesota where my family of four were all born. My parents moved away when I was two years old so I don't remember ever living there, however, we visited quite often when I was a child. My favorite maternal aunt still lived in this small town, having retired there after selling her nearby farm where she had lived for decades. I asked her to drive me around to different spots that my parents had talked about and that I had seen earlier. When she drove me by her old farm I was quite taken aback. Instead of a white house and outbuildings, as well as a red barn, all had been painted a carnival of colors. My aunt said that a Mexican family had moved into the buildings and that the land was purchased by a company. This is what started me off on the story which is fictional in all regards, even the color of the buildings, but it came from asking myself: "What if?"*

# *Carnival of Colors*

Published by *STORGY Magazine*, February 2018

She'd painted the buildings bright white, posted signs, and advertised in county newspapers as well as the Minneapolis *Star Tribune,* that the farm was for sale. 1970. A new decade. She felt ready to start a new life.

Her only offer for the land came from Midwest Farmlands, Inc. Trembling as she signed the papers, her mind filled with Gregory's mortified expression.

Weeks later, a dusty pickup rolled onto the weeping willow-bordered, gravel driveway. A vaguely familiar fellow got out. His grayed hair looked as if spatters of paint had fallen upon it. Lines etched his tan-without-the-sun face.

He gave a slight bow. "Senora Rasmussen?"

"Yes, that's me."

"I know you, I believe."

Suddenly recognizing him, she said, "You're the boy from the Memorial Carnival all those years ago."

"Si. Carlos Rivera. You're the same pretty-as-a-rosebud, golden-haired girl."

This kind of flowery talk bewildered her. Gregory had considered her to be nice looking. He used to say, "This'll look real good on you," when giving her a new beige or gray dress.

"I bring men to the Red River Valley from Mexico each spring for working the sugar beets." The man humbled his tone, "I wish to purchase your buildings to accommodate them."

*What would people think?* She led him through the house, anyway, stopping to describe different areas. Upstairs, she said, "This is the main bedroom," with an offhand gesture toward the white comforter-covered double bed. "You and your wife could sleep here."

"I have no wife." His animated face went as blank as a fallow field.

Gregory also would have thought the transaction that followed inappropriate, like overalls at a wedding or funeral. However, with no other options, Martha Rasmussen sold her buildings to Carlos Rivera, and before he took possession, she bought a little white house in nearby Chambers, Minnesota, town of 2,500.

***

Opening day of the 1943 Memorial Carnival, Martha Larkin stood at the midway watching a group of migrant workers playing a ring-toss game. The winner's dark good looks spoke to her of exotic places. He accepted a pink teddy bear, scanned the crowd, settled upon her, and sauntered over.

"I'm Carlos," he announced. "May I please present you with this gift?" His black-as-a-wishing-well eyes widened.

"Oh...I'm Martha, but I couldn't accept it." Heat rose from the tips of her toes upward as she turned away.

He stuck the teddy bear under his arm and fell into step next to her.

Soon, Martha found herself led to the dance tent, and cajoled into twirling dizzying circles to Ole Olson's Polka Band.

As the music came to a close, Carlos pulled her close and whispered, "You missed our Cinco de Mayo Festival."

She breathed in his scent of Brilliantine, wondering what he meant.

Older ladies from the Chambers Lutheran Church, like judges at the kids' talent show, scrutinized them.

Martha chose to ignore these ladies.

Her days spent with boring-as-church-sermon tasks left plenty of time for daydreams. While her parents ran Larkin's Five and Dime, Martha cared for her two younger brothers, cooked, and did housework. Her mother preferred standing at a cash register and endlessly chattering with anyone who tarried. Her father stocked shelves and ignored their weed-filled yard. Many nights they failed to come home, rather carousing at Poppy's Tavern.

After that polka, Carlos and Martha strolled around the carnival grounds. He surprised her by taking a hand in his warm one. Behind the Flag Pavilion he challenged her shyness with a forbidden kiss.

The next Monday, between errands, Martha stopped by Shirmer's Drugs and Fountain for a chocolate phosphate, imagining another meeting with Carlos Rivera. While sipping the fizzy, sweet liquid, she sensed someone approaching. Hoping she'd conjured him up, Martha nudged the revolving stool around and saw Gregory Rasmussen, who hadn't been drafted, gossips said, due to flat feet.

"Mind if I join you?" He sat down like an entitled town official.

"You have." She knew him slightly as an occasional customer at the Five and Dime.

Milly Banks ambled over and reached for a pencil tucked in her pinkish-gray bun.

"What she's having." Gregory pointed at Martha's drink, and commenced to tell her about coming back to Chambers for a long visit. With hair the color of tan linoleum, and thirty years old, his clear blue eyes proved to be as easy to read as letters on the church's welcoming sign. When she dug in her purse to pay for the phosphate, he grabbed the bill. "I'll get it."

Martha politely thanked him and headed toward the door.

"Be seeing you soon," he called after her.

Walking the few blocks back to the Larkin house, Martha moved Carlos' face over for Gregory's no-nonsense, Norwegian features. Smiling at the prospect of two interesting men, when most had been sent off to fight the war, she tiptoed onto the cement path, trying to avoid cracks. In the front hall she greeted her two brothers.

Together, they said, "Mom and Dad are at Poppy's."

A frown crumpled Martha's even features. She wanted to answer a letter from her pen pal, Lina Martinez, who lived in California, but she couldn't let the boys go hungry. Whipping up a meatloaf, she managed to push to the back of her mind drinking that would take place at the tavern, reasoning, *They are grown-ups.*

About half past eleven, after long since tucking the boys into bed and collapsing on a rocking chair, she dozed over her letter. A knock came at the front door. With no hesitation, she answered it. In Chambers nothing more notable than a tractor stalling outside the town hall ever happened.

Sheriff Johnson stood under the porch light, hat in hand. "I'm so sorry. There's been an accident." He brushed the felt brim as if to make sure it was free of dust.

***

For many months after the 10 pm train from The Cities crashed into her father's old Ford, Martha prayed for sleep, while her parents intruded, laughing and smelling of beer, with her mother urging, "You can make it..." even though red lights flashed.

The undertaker had kept their coffins closed, saying, "Nothing much I could do with the mangled bodies."

A joint funeral took place in the white clapboard Lutheran church that her parents had seldom entered. Martha always took the boys to Sunday School, which she'd also been recruited to teach. There were no close relatives, so the filled sanctuary held a mishmash of townsfolk, mostly friends from Poppy's.

Poppy herself, wore a red silk blossom bobbing on her massive bosom. She said, "We sorely miss your dear parents. Please stop by."

Martha nodded, vowing, *I'll never set foot in that place.*

Days later, several church ladies called on her to see about care for the boys. They peered into spotless corners.

"I've graduated and I'm eighteen years old. I can handle matters fine," Martha assured them.

A long-time salesclerk soon after contracted to buy the Five and Dime.

Carlos Rivera stood on the front porch one afternoon. "Will you accompany me to the carnival again...for more dancing...to raise your spirits after this great tragedy?"

She pictured the pink teddy bear resting on her pillow, but declined his invitation.

Along came Gregory Rasmussen another day, filling the front porch with his presence. "You must let me help."

"Why? You're not family."

"Felt neighborly."

"Neighborly?"

"I bought some land a few miles from here."

"What about The Cities?"

"Tired of working indoors."

Gregory leaned down and drew her to him.

Martha inhaled the smell of laundry soap, and relaxed into the safety of his strong arms.

The next day, she took the grieving boys to the month-long carnival.

Carlos approached as she bought three candied apples.

"Will you please ride with me on the carousel?" Multicolored ponies spun by in a blur.

The older boy said, "We can take care of ourselves."

She moved toward Carlos, but then thought of Gregory and his land and inched back. "We're leaving."

They hustled away with the younger boy fussing, "Just got here!"

"I'll take you to the matinee instead. *The Wizard of Oz* is playing."

She began to imagine how more than a hug would feel with a grown man like Gregory.

The carnival's last day, Martha walked with him toward the Home Crafts Exhibit. Milly Banks greeted them with a look of suspicion crossing her rouged face.

Soon after, Martha stopped by Shirmer's and Milly told her, "You be careful of that Rasmussen fellow. I saw him in The Cities with a bleached blonde. Not natural like yours."

Once they'd had a few dates, Gregory said, "You're everything I've ever wanted. I love your innocent ways." Plans began for a wedding at the Lutheran church, after he said, "You must bring your brothers to live in my new house...'til they're full grown."

***

When completed, it was a two-story white clapboard. Before long, Gregory had built a chicken coop, pig shed, and large barn. All painted white.

"Why not a red barn?" she asked.

"I like my buildings bright and white and pure. Like you."

Their honeymoon trip to Moorhead efficiently answered Martha's questions about married life. Still, sometimes those old daydreams about a different sort of being surfaced. But, she learned to shoo them away, concentrating on folding towels, scrubbing the floors, stirring a kettle of chicken dumpling soup.

Gregory possessed an instinct for farming, and he provided enough money to care for the boys, in addition to the blessing of two sons. There also was enough extra for him to occasionally buy her some simple piece of jewelry bearing a religious emblem, like a cross or a dove. She'd thank him with a big hug, hoping for extra attention that night.

Days rolled along without much disruption until Gregory took sick with what doctors called pancreatic cancer. Not sure of its location in his body, from their expressions Martha knew that soon she would be back in charge. By this time, her unmarried sons and brothers had moved to The Cities where they all worked at a sugar crystallization plant.

Diagnosed on a Friday, Gregory departed on a Wednesday, mere weeks later. His last morning, lying in their double bed under the white comforter, he strained to say, "You're young. I 'spect you'll marry again. Choose wisely." And, after a pause to summon his strength, he mumbled, "The buildings need painting before you sell."

Within hours, she quietly sang his favorite song, "From this valley they say you are going..." as Gregory passed. She closed his sunken eyes and waited, holding his scratchy, work-worn hand until a tremor shook her as he crossed over.

After the funeral, Martha awoke one morning and drove to Chambers hardware store where she bought plenty of white paint.

Gregory had wanted her to hire a few men, but this was the least she could do for him, she decided, with no idea it would take three summers to complete. The whole time, his dog, Shep, curled up in the grass, solemnly watching.

*\*\*\**

Shortly after the move to her very own house in town, late one evening while watching the news, Martha's phone rang.

"This is Carlos."

"Mr. Rivera...I hope everything's all right."

"You must visit."

"Why's that?"

"To see the changes. I want your...approval."

"That's not necessary."

"It is."

"Okay. I'll drive out tomorrow."

"No. I will gather you at noon. You must stay for a meal."

Bemused, Martha hung up.

*\*\*\**

"Please, I am Carlos." He helped her into his pickup, with a smile that turned up on one side like he had some secret to share.

"Then you call me Martha."

"Martha. It is like the wind whispering through the willows."

"Really?"

"Most decidedly."

Carlos talked with enthusiasm about how much his workers appreciated their new living arrangement. Yet, a quarter mile from the farm, his face turned wary, and he pulled to the side of the road. "It will seem strange."

"I'm sure it'll be fine."

Rolling into the driveway, a myriad of colors splashed before her eyes. The house was bright pink and chartreuse. The chicken coop was yellow and orange. The pig shed was green and red. The barn was purple. Even the windmill was turquoise. It felt like entering a carnival.

"Your men have been busy with more than beets!"

"What are your thoughts?"

"I've never seen anything like this."

"You have never visited Mexico." He leaned out the pickup window and patted a collie that put its front paws on the running board. "Do you like it?"

"It takes my breath away."

"This is good?"

"It's good." Martha recalled worried glances from the women and furrowed stares from the men when she recently entered church. Maybe they figured she'd be devastated by the changes at her old farm. Maybe they thought this served her right, for selling to outsiders. "It's beautiful!"

Reassured, Carlos brightened. "Time for tacos."

"Tacos?"

"You will like them."

They went into the spicy-smelling, goldenrod-colored kitchen. His dog trotted past Martha and headed straight for a cushion.

This took her aback. *Animals belong outside.*

Carlos served the meal, and after a couple bites, Martha said, "These are tasty," as shredded cheese spilled onto her plate.

"Messy, heh?"

"A bit." She sipped at what he called "sangria" from a green stemmed glass, and began to giggle. She stepped over and petted the collie who leaned into her touch.

"Amigo likes you."

After eating, they meandered out for a closer look at the buildings with the dog following them.

"The best is the barn," Martha said. "It reminds me of lilacs."

"I will plant bushes for you."

She tilted her head quizzically.

***

When they reached her front door, Carlos said, "You must join me for dinner on Saturday."

Martha pondered this. Then, "I'd like to."

That night, she went onto the back porch and coaxed Shep inside. He sniffed at the old blanket bunched in a corner of her bedroom, circled a few times, and flopped down upon it

Martha began to see Carlos every weekend. He picked her up, smelling of Brilliantine, and they went to community festivals, including the Chambers' Memorial Carnival. With no other couples like them, there were plenty of stares, which they disregarded, being so full of their own banter.

Once she invited him to dinner. She served her usual company lutefisk and buttered potatoes and turnips with lefse on the side.

"I apologize for the meal's whiteness."

"I will teach you some of my mother's dishes. An abundance of color and taste."

A month passed, when, with uncharacteristic reticence, Carlos said, "This Saturday I am going to Moorhead for an overnight to check on fields. Might you go with me?"

Martha recalled that skin-to-skin tingling like gentle electrical shocks. She hesitated. *What would Gregory think?*

"You do not have to make this trip. I will return on Sunday."

"No! I want to be with you."

\*\*\*

That first time, Carlos whispered, "Slower...much slower."

With his exuberant ways, she'd expected his lovemaking to be the same. Instead, he behaved as if they could lie in each other's arms forever, and her pleasure increased with subsequent visits to their hotel. When they weren't idly talking, the excitement would start, like a long ride on a Ferris wheel. Round and round and round. Soaring to the top. Gazing across a star-studded sky, with a multitude of blue, green, red lights. And, a final explosion of white as they plummeted to earth.

\*\*\*

Soon, it was time to prepare for his journey back to Mexico. On their last Saturday night, Carlos twisted a curl of Martha's hair. As she cuddled closer, he said, "You must return with me."

No matter how much she dreaded his departure, Martha had never considered this. "How can I?"

"You have no family here."

"It's my home. You stay. Go when it's time to gather your workers together."

"My mother and father are old." He dropped the curl of hair and sat up. "Maybe I will not be able to return. We will marry upon our arrival. I will care for you in the way of Gregory."

Martha hesitated a moment before saying, "I want to stay here"

They slept fitfully, and in the morning skipped their lovemaking. He was quiet on the drive back, and she pressed her lips together, trying not to weep.

Carlos finally spoke as he turned into the farm's driveway. "I will give you mementos."

There were spices for Mexican food, a gold locket with his photo, and a multicolored quilt that his mother had made.

She had nothing to give to him except a long, fierce hug.

Leaving for town, she gazed at the lilac bushes he had planted. They might very well bloom by the following year's Memorial Carnival.

***

On the Sunday after Carlos left, Martha attended church. Several ladies, now old friends, greeted her, conspicuously not mentioning all the missed services, rather asking what she wanted to make for the next week's potluck.

"Enchiladas."

They registered surprise, and one said, "What are enchi...?"

"En-chi-la-das. Spicy. Different. You'll like them."

"Bring your tuna noodle casserole," another blurted out. "Everyone loves it."

Returning to her little house, Martha felt empty, like a canister with the last remnants of sugar clinging to its sides. She walked through the rooms, reaching her double bed where his mother's multicolored quilt rested atop the white comforter. Bending down, she patted Shep, who rubbed his head against her hand.

By the following Saturday the yard was dotted with fallen leaves, but the sun streamed through a window as Martha savored her breakfast of huevos rancheros. She skipped making the casserole because she'd decided to skip church. Instead, she drove to Moorhead and bought paint. Bright pink for the siding, chartreuse for the trim, and lilac purple for her front door. She hurried home and brushed a splotch of each color on her house to get a feel for what would be the stunning results.

Standing by herself, Martha took in the vibrancy...as a surge of happiness filled her being...as she began to transform each wood slat to the liveliest of pink shades.

## A FEW FINAL WORDS

Fiction writing is a magical process. This is why I love it so much. I never know what will spark my imagination and where it will go once the process begins. I usually start out hand writing whatever it is that has grabbed my attention (the person, or event, or place) in my daily journal and then, if it seems like a story possibility, I change to a yellow notepad. Eventually, I feel ready to type the material out and finally run a first copy. I call this my "Discovery Draft."

Sometimes the initial idea doesn't go very far. I lose interest or another idea feels more important. I place those early, incomplete efforts in a file to perhaps check out at some later date. Sometimes the idea sticks with me for a long time, through many re-writes, until I finally have a story that makes sense to me and might get published and make sense to readers.

The point is, this is how my fiction develops. While some elements come from my real life, the vast majority of the words are bits and pieces of activities I've done and observations I've made that happen to fit into the plot and themes of the story. It's a mishmash of innumerable sources. Real life cannot be packaged up in a way that makes complete sense. A fictional story can.

One of the most interesting aspects of fiction writing is when a mysterious character comes along whom I can't identify in any way. That character might take over a story and I choose to let this happen. They provide insight and meaning for what I'm writing, as well as clues to my own evolving psyche.

I hope this collection, along with notes on where the stories came from, is informative for readers as well as other fiction writers.

## ACKNOWLEDGMENTS

Thank you to all the teachers from my past. There are too many to note here, but they are in my heart. Some have been forgotten, only to have their words surface at just the right time, filling me with gratitude as I recall names and faces.

I hope that my words in this collection will inspire other writers searching for stories that need only an image or two, a spark, in order to burst into flame.

## OTHER WORKS

*Making It Work* (a novel)

Santa Fe Trilogy

Made in the USA
Middletown, DE
26 September 2018